This book is dedicated to my mother, Mausty Carty, the most beautiful woman in the world.

© Copyright 2003 Austin G. Carty. All rights reserved.

No part of this publication may be reproduced, stored in a retrieval system, or transmitted, in any form or by any means, electronic, mechanical, photocopying, recording, or otherwise, without the written prior permission of the author.

Printed in Victoria, Canada

Cover painting by Mona Lisa 2003

This book was published *on-demand* in cooperation with Trafford Publishing.
On-demand publishing is a unique process and service of making a book available for retail sale to the public taking advantage of on-demand manufacturing and Internet marketing. **On-demand publishing** includes promotions, retail sales, manufacturing, order fulfilment, accounting and collecting royalties on behalf of the author.

Suite 6E, 2333 Government St., Victoria, B.C. V8T 4P4, CANADA
Phone   250-383-6864   Toll-free   1-888-232-4444 (Canada & US)
Fax   250-383-6804   E-mail   sales@trafford.com
Web site   www.trafford.com   TRAFFORD PUBLISHING IS A DIVISION OF TRAFFORD HOLDINGS LTD.
Trafford Catalogue #03-1601   www.trafford.com/robots/03-1601.html

10   9   8   7   6   5   4   3

Acknowledgements

First and foremost, I would like to thank the Lord Jesus Christ: the author and finisher of my faith.

Mom, this book was written for you, and I hope you are pleased with its final form. I love you so much. You will forever be my "best girl."

Dad and Elizabeth, I love you so much.

Special thanks to Robbie, Mike, Carson, Hopper, Kevin, Antoine, Patrick, Chase, Kevin, and Brentley for the simple service of having been my friends.

Collin Mascagni- This book would have never been written if it weren't for your encouragement to stick with my writing. Thank you for your confidence in me.

Mona Lisa Wyatt- Thank you for your finishing touch. The cover speaks volumes about your talent.

Danielle Caldwell and Dottie Hoots- I can't thank you enough for offering your time to help edit my work.

One person has stood beside me in this project from the first draft to the final copy, and I can't thank her enough. Erin Fedas, your brilliance outshines even your beauty and I can't tell you how blessed I am to call you my best friend. Thank you for seeing me as more than a mere dreamer. I love you.

Finally, I must thank my hero and the man I aspire to be:

Grandpa- I can't tell you how thankful I am for everything you have ever done for me. You truly are the standard as to who I one day hope to become. I love you. And that goes double for you, Grandma!

For those of you who are kind enough to read this book, it is my prayer that it will be as enjoyable an experience for you as writing it was for me. May the Lord bless you all.

Somewhere Beyond Here

July 8, 2066

Dearest Tyson,

As you find yourself reading this letter, I want to first congratulate you on your high school graduation. This is no small achievement young man, do not take it lightly. Though I have been gone for nearly ten years now, I pray you know how proud I am of you in spirit. I am truly sorry I could not be there to watch. —Now, on to the purpose of the enclosed:

While laying on my death bed, many years ago, my mind was filled with many wonderful memories of a life lived to its fullest. Among these fond memories, were the fireside, man- to man talks we used to have. I'll never forget the way you would listen intently to my stories, the way you would hang on my every word. Though only age three, it was quite evident you were an exceptionally smart young man. As I compose this letter, it is my hope you remember these talks as well as I do, but I understand if they are now only but a distant memory of what once was.

We would sit and talk for hours, Tyson. As you would ask me questions about the world, I would stare into your eyes, and I would see the same vigor for life that radiated from my very own. Of the stories I would tell you, there was one that you always asked me to recount. You were only a toddler at the time, and the version you remember hearing, that is, if you even remember at all, was certainly the abridged. However, I knew that one day, you would be the one in whom I would entrust the complete story. That day is now, Tyson. You are officially a man, and with that, carry the responsibility of behaving like one.

This is more than just a story, Tyson. This is the key to living life to it's fullest. This is not for you to share with the world. It is not for publication. This is the sacred story of a very special time in my life. It is my prayer that you too can learn from it the most important lesson in life. My hopes are high that you will select a special person to share it with someday, and as the light dims on his life, he too can hand it down to a loved one of his own.

It is in your hands, Tyson. Live, laugh, and love. I am forever proud of you.

Grandpa Taylor

Somewhere Beyond Here
by

Gray Leighton Taylor

Prologue: Clinging to a Promise
May, 2059

It is hard to believe I am once again attempting to write a novel. It is even harder to believe I am attempting to rewrite the exact novel I left unfinished so many years ago. But time waits for no man, and lately it has been especially unkind to me. My fingers ache as they touch these keys, yet I must press on because this is not just a book. This is a promise of sorts; a promise I made to a very special woman, nearly half a lifetime ago.

My name is Gray Taylor. I am not in any way a special man, only a man once put in a special position. I have lived what one might call "a good life," but I will certainly not be remembered when I am gone. And this thought comforts me. I lived, I loved, and I will soon say good-bye, and I will be on my way. However, I have one matter of business left on this earth, and I pray the proper words will find my fingertips, as I attempt to reveal my story.

I am not proud to admit it, but I lived a great deal of my life a cynical man. Though not a topic on which I like to dwell, I feel it in order to provide a bit of background on myself before beginning.

Sunrays danced upon my bedroom window in my youthful days. I would arise to the fresh smell of a Southern breeze blowing in the world just outside. I'd rise from my bed with big eyes and a hopeful heart, waiting to greet the world with a loving embrace. My glass was always half full.

Then tragedy struck, as does in life. But I did not understand this, for I had yet to be exposed to the lesson of loss. While living in my perfect world, I had never witnessed the fragility of life.

My father and sister were killed in a car accident in late November 2001.

Suddenly, the entire way I looked at life was altered. A God who I believed had stationed angels around my loved ones, had let two of the most important people in my life die at the hands of a drunken fool.

I had been praying one simple prayer since I was old enough to comprehend its meaning: "May God station His angels around Mommy, Daddy, and Sis." When they were killed, I knew beyond a shadow of a doubt that my prayers had been in vain.

That night, I found myself facing the most difficult decision of my life.

You see, at this point I was engaged to the young lady I had been courting since eighth grade. We were set to move to Boston the following summer, to follow her dreams of being a successful attorney. I loved her. I loved her more than life itself. But I had made a promise to another lady long before.

When I was six years old I made a solemn vow to my mother. I promised her that she would always be my best girl. So as I watched multiple sclerosis continue to limit her ability to function, I knew she could never be alone.

I gave my fiancée an ultimatum. I told her I was staying with my mother and watching over her until her final day. And I told her that if she truly loved me, she'd stay with me and that we'd live out our lives in North Carolina. That summer, my fiancée purchased a one-way ticket to Boston, Massachusetts.

Soon thereafter, love was an emotion I simply refused to experience. Bitterness had filled my heart, and I knew for certain that God didn't exist.

But there was always my mom. There always had been, and there always would be. We had a bond. It was not your normal, mother-son bond. We had a true, loving, and eternal bond.

Not a day goes by that I don't close my eyes and remember when I was a toddler, when I would wake up and run to her room, where she sat awaiting me. She would hug me. We would embrace for minutes at a time. And then we'd play. The entire day we'd play together, just she and I.

And I grew.

Sometimes in dreams I see the look in her eyes as she dropped me off my first day of school. I remember closing the door to her car, asking her timidly, if there were going to be any black children in my class. And as surely as I remember asking the question, I remember her answer. She smiled and said, "I hope so. There is nothing different between a white person and a black person, Gray. God loves us all the same, and so should you."

And I grew.

There are moments when I remember crying in her arms as my first girlfriend broke up with me in middle school. I recall how being in her arms made me feel protected and loved. It eased my burden. That's what she always did, eased my burdens when I was weak.

And I grew.

Some nights when I cry, reflecting on how proud I am of my own children, I understand the abundance of tears my mother shed at my high school graduation. Her tears were of humility. She was humbled, realizing how magnificent a God she served, allowing her to have a child who loved her so much.

And still I grew.

There are times I remember embracing with tears in our eyes the day she found out she had multiple sclerosis. In my heart I can still feel the ache from that moment. The memory of that moment left a scar that time will never fade.

All the while, I grew.

I will never mistake the difference between her tears at my graduation and the tears she shed the day she said goodbye to me my freshman year of college. The tears that day were tears of sorrow. Though I couldn't grasp the extremity of the situation, she, being older and wiser, could. We would never be able to relive the days that had just passed. I was now a grown man, and I was opening my wings for the first time, flying away to a whole new life.

Some nights I am haunted by the pain I saw in her eyes the night my father and sister died. I lie still in my bed gasping for breath and begging for the shadows that crawl along my wall to ease up and let a squint of light illuminate the photograph of her I have by my bed. Then I am able to see her smile.

I recall how she held me the morning after the break up with my fiancée, just as she had after my first break up. I remember how she promised me that we'd beat everything together and vowed that we'd be all right. I still marvel at her strength.

I remember how it hurt to watch as she climbed into her wheelchair for the very first time. I can remember how apparent her pain was but how she refused to relinquish her smile.

Finally, I remember finding out why she could no longer digest her meals properly. Every day I ask God's forgiveness for my behavior as I coped with her cancer. Luckily, He always reminds me of the final act she performed before slipping into her coma: with weariness evident in her eyes, she gripped my hand a little tighter, and smiled.

That smile took place nearly a half century ago, yet it fuels my fire each and every day.

Yes, I remember.

It was she who brought me into this world, and it was I who saw her out. She taught me life, she taught me death, and in between, she taught me the most important lesson of all: she taught me love.

As I inch closer to the finish of my own life, I cling tighter to the memory of her. Though sometimes I feel sadness, I usually feel humility, for as I stated earlier, I have lived a good life. But in these times of mourning and self-pity, I simply look to the sky and pick a star. My eyes shut and my mind goes blank, and suddenly, I am reminded of a song.

A Simple Song
October 27, 1986

He stared off distantly into space, trying to block out the whiney noises coming from the room beside him. The little baby's screams had grown quite intolerable to say the least. The familiar nurturing voice of his mother rang through his ears. He despised the fact that the familiarity now came from listening to her comfort the new addition instead. He sighed with despair.

Gray Taylor had grown quite accustomed to being the apple of his mother's eye. Since he had been in this world, Sylvia Taylor had spoiled him rotten. Love, hugs, and kisses were the backbone of their relationship. Spending every waking minute of every single day playing games, running errands, and putting together jigsaw puzzles was understood to be the daily routine. However, a new little creature had decided to come out of mommy's tummy, and now those days seemed to be a distant memory. Such a thought made Gray Taylor's life a complete blur of sadness. He had been replaced.

"Honey, come here!" Sylvia called for her husband, Jack Taylor, to come to the baby's room. He was busily watching football in the living room.
"Can't, babe; the Skins are down three with forty-five seconds left—but we're driving!"
"Honey, you've got to come here; she just laughed for the first time!"

Gray listened to this dialogue, and was overcome with shock as he heard his father get up from his recliner and run into the baby's room. He had been living in the house for five and a half years. He knew that there were very few things that could arouse his father from his recliner and Washington Redskin football. Damn that little brat.

"You see, if you just give her a tiny tickle, she starts giggling so hard that her little legs start kicking."

Jack smiled at his wife. "Look at how adorable she is; she's certainly got her mother's smile!"

"Yessy mommy's little baby girl, yes you are, yes you are. Mommy loves you. That's right, she does. Mommy loves her little angel!"

All the baby talk was enough to make Gray's blood boil with rage. Though the tickling and the excessive attention that the baby stole from Gray was quite enough, the silly love jibber-jabber containing those exact words was an exclusive. The phrase was, and always had been, "mommy's little baby *boy*." Now the little brat had even stolen that.

He buried his face in his pillow, and closed his eyes, dreaming of the times when he was the object of attention in the Taylor household.

Suddenly, he heard footsteps coming down the hallway of their little one story house. The house was nearly seventy years old, and none of the previous inhabitants had taken the initiative to modify the floors. Therefore, when someone walked through the house, every footstep could be heard. The steps Gray heard were light- certainly his mother's- and they were directed toward his room.

His mother softly knocked on his door before opening it and peeking inside. Gray attempted to mask his melancholy status, but the attempt was weak. For needless to say, how can one who feels so rejected hide such a feeling? Sylvia picked up on it immediately.

Gray was her first-born, her first priority; he was the apple of her eye. The days they had spent together since he had been born were the happiest of her life. The thought that she was causing such sadness to him crushed her. Luckily, she had a plan.

"Hey, honey," she said as she walked over to his bed.
"Hey, Mommy." His monotone reply, which was muffled with a plea for love and attention, caused Sylvia to flash one of her golden smiles his way. Her smile always had a way of lifting his spirits.
"Claire laughed for the first time just a minute ago."
"Really?" Gray pretended that he didn't already know and, meanwhile, pretended that he cared.
"Uh huh," she said, nodding her head, "it was the cutest little thing. Her little legs

kicked as she tried to squirm away from our fingers."

Gray didn't reply.

"Listen, honey. How about you and I go to a movie?"

Gray immediately jumped from his bed. "Really? - Just you and me?"

"Just you and me, my little queege."

Sylvia had been calling him her "little queege" for three and a half years now, because when he was first learning to talk, he would attempt to ask his mother to "squeeze" him in a loving embrace. However, he could not pronounce "squeeze," so " queege" is what came out. Sylvia thought it was the most precious thing in the world.

Gray leaped off his bed and ran to his closet where he grabbed his coat and winter cap. Sylvia smiled as she watched the excitement in the young boy.

"Button it!" she directed as she motioned toward the jacket. "And make sure and pull that cap over your ears. It's cold out there!"

Gray heeded the instructions and then looked up at his mother as if to ask, "Can we go now?"

She smiled and nodded toward the door. The boy ran out of his room and down the creaky hallway to tell his father the big news of where he was going- and more importantly, where the new nuisance wasn't.

As they parked the car in the *Clover Leaf* grocery store parking lot, adjacent to the newly built cinema, Sylvia looked over at Gray and told him to hold his rush to exit the car.

"There's someth ing I want to talk to you about, Gray."

The boy looked up at his mother with concerned eyes. "What is it, Mommy?"

"Well, it's about Claire." She paused to gather her thoughts. "About the amount of time I have been spending with her."

Gray frowned.

"I k now it's not fair to you, honey, but you have to let me explain. Little babies are very delicate. You have to nurture them with so much love and attention. When a little baby, like your sister, comes into this world, they are completely helpless. They need food at the strangest times of the day. They cry at the silliest things; and the reason they do this, is because they are trying to make sense out of this new place they have stumbled upon."

She looked over to see if he was following. "Is this making any sense?"

Gray nodded.

"So when I am spending all of this time with Claire and laughing and playing with her, it doesn't mean that I love her more than you, or that I would rather be with her. It simply means that I am having to work extra hard to help her grow up to be as sweet a person as you are."

Gray smiled in an earnest way of saying, "Thank you."

"So can you forgive me?"

"Yes, Mommy."

"Are you still my little queege?"

"Yes, Mommy."

"Am I still always going to be your best girl?"

Gray nodded, remembering his promise that she would forever be his "best girl."

"You will always be my best girl Mommy," he said with a sheepish look on his face. Sylvia's heart melted.

The movie they were set to see was an animated movie that Sylvia had heard nothing but good reviews about. As she watched the movie, Sylvia couldn't believe how touched she was. The movie did such a great job of depicting the love amongst a tightly knit family. She constantly looked over to watch Gray's reactions. The boy sat on the edge of his seat the entire movie, hanging on every word each character delivered. As the movie finally concluded to the score "Somewhere Beyond Here," mother and son were both in tears.

The two sat still in the theater until the song ended. Then, only empty popcorn boxes, a screen filled with credits, and Sylvia and Gray remained in the theater. Finally, they stood and walked out.

As they got in the car and started driving, Sylvia looked to Gray.

"Did you listen to the words of that song, Gray?"

He nodded his head, signaling "yes."

"It said:

Somewhere beyond here, amidst the shining stars,

Someone's watching over me, watching from afar.
Somewhere beyond here, someone's resting in God's arms, asking Him to bless me and keep me safe from harm.
Somewhere beyond here, where angels dry your tears, someone's waiting for me, somewhere beyond here."

The boy looked up at his mother with big eyes.

"Gray, one day, when Jesus calls Mommy away from this world, and we aren't able to see one another anymore, I want you to know that I'll be looking down on you, loving you so much and being so proud of you. And when you miss me, you will always be able to think of that song and know that it is our song. And you will remember this promise for the rest of your life. Okay?"

"What do you mean when you're not here anymore, Mommy?"

"Well, baby, Jesus has a plan for all of us. And in His perfect plan, all people must eventually die and go on to be with Him forever."

"But, Mommy, I don't want you to die."

"I know yo u don't honey, but it's something in nature that can't be avoided."

Gray started to cry. Death was a thought he had never pondered.

"But I will miss you, Mommy!"

"And I will miss you, Sweetheart. But you will always have that song to remember, and know that I will be smiling down on you from heaven, beaming with pride at the fine young man you have become."

"I'm not going to let you die, Mommy— Ever!"

Sylvia fought back tears and forced a smile, realizing that her son loved her so much he thought he could find a way to overcome death so that she could be with him forever. She smiled at him. "I love you so much, honey."

"I love you too, Mommy."

A Deadly Sin
Late December, 2002

Gray Taylor watched his breath as it escaped from his mouth into the harsh winter air, before finally evaporating into nothingness. The ground was cold on his rear as he sat in waiting. He grabbed at the pack of cigarettes in his back pocket, but then thought the better of the idea. If the man was to come back in the next five minutes, he may catch a glimpse of the smoke coming from behind the bushes. He shoved the pack back in his jeans.

His aluminum baseball bat was freezing his fingertips, and he could sense the digits were dangerously close to becoming numb. He released the weapon and let it lie dormant on the ground. He briskly rubbed his hands together, hoping the friction would produce some warmth to combat the arctic temperature. He frowned at the thought of how cold this winter had been in the Carolinas.

Other than the steady sound of winter wind, the only sounds to be heard were of the occasional cars rolling home at the late hour. He judged that the majority of these were men either coming home from the bar or coming home from sleeping with someone other than their spouse; a meeting made possible by the convenient lie, "I was working late."

There were no lights on in the house he was studying. He couldn't have asked for a more perfect arrangement. The neighborhood was dead, and the only link to family that the asshole had was his son, who apparently was with his mother tonight. There was no one was stirring in the house.

There was the possibility the little kid was with his father, and that would completely ruin Gray's plans. He contented himself in the hope that this would not be the case.

An itch nagged at his lower left calf, so he squatted down in order to scratch it. Just as he had balanced himself for the remedy, headlights motioned toward the house from down the road. He gave a quick scratch to the irritation and remained perfectly still in his squatted position, poised to carry out that which he had come here to do.

As the light drew closer, finally coming within fifteen yards of his spot, the car applied brakes and turned into the driveway. Soon, the engine died and the lights faded into extinction. As the truck door opened, the service light illuminated the man's face. Despite the freezing temperature, Gray felt his face grow red with anger. As the man shut the door and turned his back to the bush where Gray was hiding, Gray reached over to the spot where his TPX little league bat was sitting. It was time.

He had planned the entire event perfectly. He would not rush the man insanely and beat him to death in his front yard. Instead, he would simply time his delicate sprint and run right in the door behind him. He would launch the surprise attack just as the door was closed. Once the door was closed, all hell would break loose for about five minutes. Then, he would never have to think of it again.

The man began walking toward his door. It became apparent very quickly to Gray that the man had been drinking.

"That son of a bitch," he thought.

With each step, Gray's heart beat a little faster. He gripped his bat more tightly. The man was nearing the four-step entrance to his doorway. As soon as he reached the second step, it was time.

Step one, step two, now.

Gray quickly, yet quietly, sprinted to the front door. Just as it was about to be shut, he forced his way through the door and shut it behind him. The shocked look on the man's face was quickly replaced by fear.

"Wai… wha… Take what you want."

The alcohol on the man's breath was sickening.

"I don't want shit from you!" Gray's voice was full of rage.

He threw a quick punch with his fist that connected square with the man's jaw. The punch sent him flying onto his back. Then slowly, Gray removed the dark mask he was wearing.

"Recognize me?"

The man's eyes widened with shock. "I… I'm sorry, Gray. Please…"

He attempted to bargain his way out of the inevitable, but none of his pleas were going to be rewarded.

"Payback's a bitch isn't it?"

Gray took his other hand and grabbed the bat. He gripped it as if he were stepping up to the plate. He first swung violently at the man's torso, not wanting to deliver the final blow too soon. He wanted the man to experience a little pain first.

The first blow connected with flesh and bone. The man screamed in agony. He attempted one final plea, but before it could run off his trembling lips, Gray's bat connected with his skull, shattering the man's cranium. Blood flew across the foyer and onto the cream-painted walls.

Gray took two extra swings to the man's head to ensure his death. Then he delivered a few final blows to the sternum out of sheer rage. With that, he took one last look at the devastation he had created and quickly turned to exit the house. After rushing to the door to wipe his fingerprints from the doorknob, he ran off into the cold winter night.

A Deep Sleep
Present Date, 2012

He held her feeble hand in his. He had become immune to the sound of the constant beeping overhead that assured him that his mother was still alive. The beeping, along with an Atlanta Braves baseball game that he was paying no attention to, were the only sounds in the room.

He stared at her face. He wished she could open her eyes. He missed the twinkle they used to project, the twinkle that radiated a sense of warmth to anyone who was blessed enough to peer inside them.

Her lips were pressed tightly together. Their once soft and vivid look now appeared lifeless and frail.

He smiled as he looked at her nose. She had always been so ashamed of it. She would constantly speak of how big it was- claiming that one could do ski-jumps off of it.

Everyone knew she was the most beautiful woman in the city. Hell, there were many that were convinced she might be the prettiest sixty-year old woman on the planet. She was, however, way too humble to ever realize the truth.

"Excuse me, Mr. Taylor," a voice said behind him.

Gray Taylor turned to face the resident nurse, Mary Thorn. He couldn't help noticing how beautiful the girl was.

"Oh, hey, Mary. Is it check-up time?"
"Check-up time."
"All right, I'm gonna go grab a smoke."
"You? Never!"
"Yeah, figured I'd start something new today. You two have fun."

Gray grabbed his jacket off the coat hanger on the wall and walked out the door. He headed down the hall and hopped into the familiar elevator.

He stood, waiting for the elevator to drop him off at his lobby area destination. As he waited, he attempted to block out the horrible elevator rendition of Elton John's "I Guess That's Why They Call It the Blues" in the background. He wondered how anyone who claimed to be a musician could destroy such a good song.

The elevator finally dinged, indicating he had arrived at the lobby. Gray walked from the elevator and nodded to Merle and Jamie who were working at the lobby reception desk. He continued walking to the door leading outside. As he walked, he thought about how odd a pairing the two were. Merle was a sixty-four-year-old black woman with two kids, an ex-husband, and a spot on the Deaconess board at her local church and Jamie was a seventeen-year-old high school junior, fresh off an abortion and a broken engagement to a thirty-one year old mechanic.

What a duo.

The doors leading out of the hospital opened as he got within five feet of them. Gray walked through them and into the cold January evening. He shivered as he zipped up his coat.

The coat was a Christmas gift he had gotten from his mother nearly twenty years earlier. It was now completely out-of-style, but his need for fashion acceptance had died long ago. Today he was a broken, confused, lonely man and had no time to worry about what society thought of his choice of clothing.

He took out his pack of cigarettes and frowned, remembering that the ignorant clerk at the 7-11 didn't listen to his instructions as to which cigarettes were his fancy. He had asked for his usual Camel Lights and somehow had ended up with Marlboros instead. He scolded himself for being too lost in thought to pay any attention to the purchase. He sighed deeply and figured, *What's the difference. They all kill you just the same.* He pulled out a stick and put it to his lips. He reached for his lighter and lit up.

"Hey, buddy," a voice came from behind him. A bit startled, Gray wheeled around. He met eyes with an elderly man who stood smiling at him.

"Can I help you?" Gray asked.

"I don't know; I guess it all depends on your answer to my question."

Gray took a drag and shrugged as he blew it out.

"Got a fag you can lend me?"

Gray cocked his eyebrow and scoffed at the comment. "Interesting terminology there, old man," he snickered as he reached into his pocket.

"Yeah, the other night I was out here bumming a rod, and you should have seen the look on the face of a guy who responded to that same question by handing me a Virginia Slim."

Gray chuckled. "You're not much of one to be politically correct, I take it."

The man smiled. "I wasn't trying to offend the guy; that's just what we always called smokes back when I was in high school. Guess the times have changed a bit since then."

Gray nodded in agreement. The old man shot him a smile. It wasn't an uncomfortable or threatening smile. Instead it was a genuine, warm smile, the type Gray hadn't seen in ages. He studied the man:

He was around 5'10," probably in his mid-to late-sixties. He had deep blue eyes, dark skin, and gray hair. He was clothed in jeans and a suede jacket that showed hints of a green and red sweater hiding beneath it. Gray figured the sweater to be a festive garment, likely still off the shelves from the Christmas holiday that had just passed.

"So, you gonna hand me one of those babies or not, son?" The old man had yet to stop smiling.

"Oh, yeah, sorry. I must have spaced out there for a second."

"No problem. What ya smokin'?"

"Marlboro Lights, unfortunately. The girl at the store handed me the wrong pack."

"Gotta hate it when that happens," the old man said as he waved his hand, turning down Gray's offer of a lighter. He reached into his pocket and pulled out a lighter of his own. He lit up and then took a drag. As he exhaled he said, "So, you gonna introduce yourself, son, or am I to believe Southern manners really did go out the window with your generation?"

Gray was no longer paying attention to the man. He was thinking about Sylvia. Upon hearing the question, he said, "I'm sorry. I'm Gray. Gray Taylor."

"Nice meeting you, Taylor," the man said as he gripped Gray's hand tightly. "The name's Rose. Colonel Rose."

Gray nodded. "I'm not supposed to salute or anything, am I?"

"No, I think the handshake will do." The Colonel laughed.

"So what brings you to this fine establishment for healing the sick and accommodating the healthy, Taylor?" The old man exhaled a smoke ring.

"My mother," Gray responded plainly.

Gray had never been open with anyone when it came to his mother's illness. Striking up a conversation about that exact thing with a stranger was an idea he was not very comfortable with.

"Sorry to hear that, son."
Gray nodded. He had become used to hearing the generic comment.
"I'm here on account of my wife."
"What's wrong with her?" Gray asked, attempting to humor the man and make casual conversation.
"Cancer."
Gray frowned. Cancer was the same illness his mother was struggling with.
"Isn't it always cancer?" the Colonel continued. "Seems everyone breathes their last on account of it these days."
Gray sighed and nodded in agreement. "My mom has cancer, too."
The Colonel paused for a moment. His eyes were fixed on Gray. He took note of his cold demeanor. Finally, he nodded and offered an apology.

"I'm sorry to hear that kid. How long has she had it?"

Without really thinking, Gray unloaded the misfortunes of his mother's health on the stranger.

"Well, when I was a little kid she was diagnosed with reynauds, which is a disease that affects her joints. A few years later, we found out she had lupus. Right before I went away to college, she found out she had multiple sclerosis."

Gray paused and took in a drag of his cigarette.

"Then, finally, the cancer came about five months ago." He sighed. "It has taken its toll quickly."

"Well, how's she taking it?"

Gray noted that for the first time he actually felt like someone had honest intentions in their line of questioning. He had never prided himself in much, but being a good judge of character was something he had always believed himself to be. This old man, he felt, seemed to be genuinely concerned about his situation.

"Well, she ha s always had a great way of facing adversity. When she first found out she had cancer, it was tough on her. The knowledge that she probably only had a few months left was hard for her to come to grips with."

Gray paused and thought for a second.

"I haven't come to grips with it though. I don't think I ever will. For over ten years now it's just been the two of us. Once she's gone, I have nobody. She's my best friend." Gray thought for a second and softly uttered, "My only friend."

He stared at the ground for a second and then snapped back to reality. "But anyway, she's in a coma, so I have no idea how she's taking it at the moment."

The Colonel stared off for a second and then met eyes with Gray. "That's tough son. I'll be praying for her."

Because Gray knew the man was being genuine, he hid the discomfort that the statement had brought him. Gray Taylor was all too familiar with religion. He was brought up in the church and had attended Christian schools. He had believed in God all of his youthful days. But somewhere along the way, God had abandoned Gray. That was the only explanation for the series of misfortunes that had plagued his life.

In order not to offend the old man, he mustered a half-smile and uttered, "Thanks."

"So what about your dad and siblings? Don't you have any family or friends? I mean, what on earth makes you think you're alone, son?"

Gray rolled his head around his neck, trying to loosen his tense muscles. He dropped the remnant of his cigarette on the ground and crumpled it with his shoe.

Before he could give a response, a beeping sounded in the Colonel's pant pocket. He reached in and pulled out a beeper.

"I didn't know they still made pagers," Gray said.

The Colonel chuckled as he checked the number. "Yeah, I just can't bring myself to rely on those cell phones. Seems they always go out of service just when someone needs to reach you the most."

Gray nodded. "You have a point there."

"Well, anyway, Taylor, I hate to run on ya, but I have some business I have to take care of."

Gray nodded his approval.

"Anyway, it was great meeting you, and I'll be praying for your mom. Remember, the Lord works in mysterious ways."

Gray laughed mockingly. "Yeah, he sure does doesn't he."

"Well, take care, kid; maybe I'll see ya around sometime soon. Thanks again for the fag." The old man smiled as he turned to walk down the street.

Gray watched him for about half a minute, then turned around and walked back toward the door. He glanced over his shoulder one final time to get one last look at the old man, but he had disappeared into the city night.

"Must have turned on Parkway," Gray concluded to himself.

He turned and walked back toward the entrance. As the motion sensors indicated he was ready, the doors split open, and he walked back into the friendly warmth of the High Point Memorial Hospital lobby.

Sweet Whisperings

Mary frowned as she reached over and touched Sylvia Taylor's lifeless hand. She glanced at the heart monitor Sylvia was hooked to, giving it the once over to ensure that all things were working properly.

Feeding time had just ended for Sylvia, and Mary glanced around the room, making sure there wasn't anything left in her routine duties that she had forgotten. She gently tucked the strands of hair that hung to the left side of her face behind her ear. Finally, she ended her daily routine the same way she always had. She glanced at the door making sure no one was set to come in, and then she hit her knees on the ground beside Sylvia's bed.

With her soft hand cupping that of Sylvia's, she lifted her voice in prayer:

"Dear God, I bring this special woman before you. I pray your will be done in her life. May your angels be stationed around her, and peace be with her internal thoughts. I also lift up her son Gray to you, Father. May he be willing to let this woman who is so special to him, go on to be with you. And most importantly, Lord, may he come to rest peacefully in the knowledge of salvation through your Son. I pray these things in Jesus' Precious Name. Amen."

She then stood and leaned over Sylvia's bed. Gently, she planted a kiss on her forehead.

Resident Nurse Mary Thorn was a remarkable woman. Though her external beauty was evident, it was her kind heart and sweet spirit that drew people to her.

She had only been a nurse for a month, and Sylvia Taylor was the first patient she was ever assigned to care for. It was evident, even to the rest of the world who had never seen her pray by Sylvia's bedside, that she had a very deep concern for Sylvia. Gray was constantly taken aback by the delicate care she provided for his mother. He was extremely thankful that such a woman was watching over her.

The first day she had walked into the hospital room, Gray took notice of her striking beauty.

She had light brown hair that was filled with radiant streaks of golden blonde. The hair fell down just below her shoulders.

Her deep blue eyes were warm and inviting.

Her skin was smooth and delicate. Though she was a bit pale at the moment, Gray could tell she most likely tanned well in the summer months.

Her height of 5'4" was short, but cute. Her height was very inviting to Gray, who himself was not a tall person.

It was apparent she either worked out or was one of those fortunate few whose body was always in shape whether she worked at it or not. Nonetheless, the package was something any man would be honored to claim as his own.

The door opened and Mary was greeted by a 'So, how's our girl looking today?"

'She's looking beautiful as ever. How was the smoke?"

Gray ignored the question. "Yep, ain't she a beaut?" He leaned over and kissed Sylvia's forehead. "Still lookin' great, Ma."

Mary smiled and headed toward the door. "Have a good night, Gray."

Gray nodded and then shot a quick question in her direction. "Hey, Mary?"

She turned to face him, her eyebrow was extended upwards.

"You by chance know a woman with the last name 'Rose?'" Gray asked.

"Rose? Like the flower?"

"Yeah, cancer patient."

Mary thought for a moment. "Doesn't ring any bells. Should it?"

"I have no idea. I just happened upon an old man downstairs whose wife is dying of cancer like Mom. It was really strange. He walked up and asked to bum a cigarette from me. I was trying to avoid talking with the guy, but then he struck up a conversation about cancer. Next thing I knew, I was telling him a little bit about Mom."

"You?" Mary was shocked at the thought of Gray opening up to *anyone* about his mother's condition, let alone a complete stranger. "Well, what all did he have to say?"

43

Gray shrugged. "Just some reassuring words and then, of course, the textbook line about prayer."

Mary frowned. "You know, prayer can be a very powerful thing, Gray."

Gray scoffed. Though he strongly disagreed, he decided getting into a religious debate was not what he was in the mood for. He blew off the comment.

"Well, anyway, just wondering if you knew her. Take care, Mary."

"You too. You sleeping here?"

Gray nodded and reached over to rub his mom's arm. "You don't think I'd leave my best girl alone now, do ya?"

Mary smiled.

"Besides, I need to be here when she snaps out of this."

Mary attempted to force another smile. It was common knowledge to all but Gray that, barring a miracle, Sylvia was never coming out of her coma.

"Goodnight, Gray.'

"Night.

An Old Flame

The LaGuardia Airport was crowded as always, and the noise of the hustle and bustle of the thousands of people heading in their separate directions seemed to personify the New York world just outside. Renee Starnes was glad this was not her final stop.

She sat still in her seat just outside the Delta Gate 4B, awaiting her flight to Atlanta. She was not pleased that her trip came complete with two layovers: her current one in New York and then one in Atlanta, before finally reaching her destination of Greensboro, North Carolina. It didn't make any sense to her why she had to fly past Greensboro and then turn right around and shoot back up.

Her *People* magazine had quickly become boring, as she had already exhausted all of the Hollywood dating gossip. Now all she had to read about were tales of what was going on in the real world, that or a segment on some athlete she had never heard of nor could care less about. She turned towards the back and contented herself to do the crossword puzzle.

Renee Starnes was Gray Taylor's ex-fiancée. The two were high school sweethearts who had continued dating through college. They were engaged close to a year after Gray's graduation, and had planned to wed the following summer. The marriage would take place right after Renee's own graduation. They terminated their engagement later that winter.

Though not flashy, she was a very attractive girl. She had naturally curly blonde hair, which she would more often than not straighten because she believed it made her look more professional.

She had blue eyes and a warm smile. All who met Renee were drawn to her.

She was a graduate of Boston University Law School and, directly following her graduation, was offered a position with Anderson, Delaney and Crawford, one of the most prestigious law firms in the city.

A hard, determined worker, Renee climbed the ladder of importance in the firm and, to the present date, was one of their top attorneys. The thought of leaving Boston and the close friends she had made was hard, but she was now on a mission. A mission of love, forgiveness and reconciliation with the one man she could ever truly love.

She glanced at her watch to see how much longer she had before departure. Realizing she still had over forty minutes, she grabbed her puzzle tighter and impatiently continued searching her mind for useless trivia. She was full of many virtues. Patience was certainly not one of them.

"Who the hell is supposed to know who played Dr. Quinn?" she thought to herself. *"The show hasn't aired in fifteen years, and no one watched it even when it did."*

"Tom Cruise's name in *Cocktail*?"

The old man sitting next to her interrupted her thought process.

"It's Flannagan."

"Excuse me?" Renee said, confused.

"It's Flannagan. Brian Flannagan was Cruise's name in Cocktail."

Taken off guard, she slowly replied, "Oh, thank you."

"Sorry, I just happened to be looking at your puzzle and saw you were struggling with that one."

Though Renee had not yet even read the full clue, she knew that even had she, she would have had no idea what the answer was. She simply nodded and said, "Well, thanks."

"It's no problem. Well, I better get going." The man stood up and walked away, disappearing amongst the continuous flow of human traffic.

Renee stared across the room at a child crying in his mother's arms. The woman made no effort to remove herself and her child, therefore allowing all of the other people stationed around them to enjoy the soothing sounds of a crying child. Renee bit her lip. Irritated, she looked back down to her puzzle and resumed killing time.

A Physician

Dr. Terry Ravel smiled as he said goodbye to Timmy Bryan. Timmy had just been given a cast for his broken leg and was on his way out of the hospital before Dr. Ravel had stopped him to make sure that everything had gone smoothly.

It was great to know that there were still doctors like Terry Ravel left in the world, the kind who weren't in practice for the paycheck. Instead, they were in it to help people.
Dr. Ravel had never met Timmy before, nor had he ever even heard mention of his name. But when he happened to cross paths with the boy, he saw the fresh cast on his leg. Without thinking, he stopped to take the time to ask him how he was feeling and tried to lift his spirit by positively reinforcing that the cast would be off in less than two months. Dr. Ravel truly was a special doctor.

He turned from where he had stood talking with Timmy and his mother, and walked down the corridor toward the elevator. He had deep issues on his mind, deepest being Sylvia Taylor. It was her room he was en route toward.

As the elevator door opened in front of him, Mary Thorn stepped off and greeted him with a cheerful, "What's up, Doc?"

"Please no Bugs Bunny from you Mary. I get that too often."

She smiled.

"Besides, you're too cute to be Bugs Bunny. You'd have to be Ariel or Princess Jasmine or someone cute like that." He smiled sheepishly.

"Easy there, Doc. You know its open season for sexual harassment suits don't you?" Mary laughed.

"Yeah, I know, but I have a good lawyer."

They both laughed, and then Mary said goodbye and turned to walk away.

"Oh, wait a minute, Mary."

Dr. Ravel had been so caught up in his harmless flirting that he had forgotten Mary was the exact person he needed to speak to.

"Yep?" Her hair flung in the wind as she whipped her body back around.

"You been to see Sylvia Taylor yet today?"

"Yes. Just coming from there as a matter of fact."

Dr. Ravel scratched his chin, rubbing the stubble that was now coming in on account of his five minutes of extra sleep. "Nothing new I presume?"

Mary frowned. "Nope. Same ol,' same ol."

Dr. Ravel nodded, suggesting he already knew what Mary's response would be. "The son in there?" he asked.

"Gray?"

Dr. Ravel nodded.

"Yeah, he just got back up there as I was leaving."

"You know the guy pretty well don't you, Mary?"

Mary thought about it for a moment. "Well, I guess you could say that. I mean, we talk a little bit every time I go in there."

Dr. Ravel nodded. "You think he feels comfortable around you?"

Mary shrugged. "I guess. We're not best friends or anything, but he seems to like me, I think," She paused for a second. "Why do you ask?"

Dr. Ravel dropped his eyes and stared at the ground for a second.

"Well, to be honest, I don't have the best rapport with him, Mary. I think he's a good guy, and naturally he loves his mother very much." He paused. "But he's so stubborn."

Mary continued listening.

"I realize that he's hostile toward me because I have to constantly suggest that he allow us to take Sylvia off life support. I know that is a tough thing to hear."

Mary nodded in agreement.

"But it's been over a month now, and she hasn't shown any sign of recovery. He has to let her go. I can't pull the plug without his permission, and each time I have talked with him, he hasn't shown any sign of changing his mind. The kid is so convinced that she is going to simply 'snap out of it,' as if it's that easy." He sighed.

"Anyway, I was wondering if maybe you could try to talk to him about it."

The thought made Mary feel a bit uneasy. "Well, I don't know, Doc, that might be pretty awkward. I…"

Dr. Ravel interrupted her. "You don't have to be forceful; just try to bring it up if you have a chance."

Mary nodded, "Okay, I'll see what I can do."

Dr. Ravel nodded appreciatively. "Thanks Mary. I have to get going. I have to go see Sylvia and then listen to Gray tell me how lousy of a doctor I am."

Mary laughed. "Good luck."

Dr. Ravel smiled, "See ya, beautiful."

"Later, Yosemite Sam."

A Flight to Remember

The aisle seat where she had been ticketed did not please Renee at all. She stared with envious eyes at the man in the cheap, Armani knockoff coat, who inhabited the window seat she longed for. If only she had that seat, she could simply have stared out at the dark evening clouds, and lost her thoughts somewhere a thousand miles above the New York skyline.

She then took note of the empty seat distancing her from the man. She decided it was a much worse location than that which she had been dealt. She could only imagine the pick- up material this want-to-be Wall Street nobody would be feeding her. Her best guess was that he was probably some form of salesman, the lowest rung of employee status in America in her opinion. Traveling salesmen always, though married, felt the need to put the moves on any attractive woman they came across on the road. She hoped the passenger who was headed for this seat wasn't a woman.

No woman should have to deal with such harassment.

"Excuse me. Pardon me. Excuse me."

She heard pleas for forgiveness nearly five aisles ahead of her as the unnamed crossword puzzle man tried to move through aisles already packed with passengers and their belongings.

"Pardon me, ma'am," he said as he accidentally caught a woman's knee with his faded canvas carry-on bag.

"*At least he has manners,*" Renee thought to herself.

He continued moving through the aisles, and it struck Renee that he could very likely be heading for the empty seat beside her. She cringed a bit and pretended to stare off into space. She hadn't planned on spending the flight having to talk, and she could tell from the two seconds she'd known this man that's exactly what he'd have in mind.

"Well, well. If it isn't my very own Elizabeth Shue," he said as he shot a smile at Renee. He reached upward and tucked his carry-on in the overhead compartment, which signaled he was, indeed, sitting in the seat beside her.

"Excuse me?" Renee said. "Elizabeth who?"

"Shue," he said nonchalantly as he removed his jacket. "Elizabeth Shue was the pretty little girl who co-starred opposite Tom Cruise in *Cocktail*." He smiled. "You really need to work on your knowledge of that one dear."

Not knowing whether to be offended or obliged, she simply nodded her head. "Oh."

"So did you get that puzzle all completed?"

Renee frowned internally as she could see that her premonitions about the man's chatty nature were being confirmed.

"No, I don't remember who played Dr. Quinn, and I have no reason to know who the star Los Angeles Raider running back whose injury forced him to retirement in the early 90's was." She offered a half smile. "Those sports questions get me every time."

The older man reciprocated with a smile of his own. However, this time, Renee took note for the first time how charming his smile was. He had a very handsome set of white teeth.

"Well I, like you and the rest of the planet, have no idea who played the part of that Medicine Woman," he said.

Renee laughed.

"I'd put a bet down that whoever she is, she's not admitting to having played her either," he chuckled. "But anyhow, Bo Jackson was the running back you speak of."

"Come again?" she said as she reached for her magazine and flipped to the page of her nearly complete crossword puzzle.

"Jackson." See if the clue doesn't have seven boxes for you.

Renee smiled realizing he was right. "Sure enough. Fits in perfectly with the 's' from *Survivor*, and the 'n' from Paul Newman." She scribbled the word in. "Thanks."

"No problem. I was always a Darryl Green fan myself, but old Bo used to light up the field before he blew his hip out."

He kept jabbering about football, but Renee had stopped paying attention to the dialogue.

"You're not listening to me, are you, dear," he said as he realized she hadn't heard a word he'd said in the last minute.

"I- I'm sorry, sir, I guess I'm just a little preoccupied."

He flashed his golden smile. "That's all right; not many women do continue listening when football is the topic." He laughed. "My wife used to hate my passion for football. Drove her insane when I'd sit at the dinner table Sunday evenings, talking about all of the touchdown runs and passes of the day," He laughed as he reminisced.

"So, what preoccupies you, dear?"

"Oh, nothing really," she said hesitantly.

"Better not be nothing," he said jokingly. "I have plenty more football stories to tell you once you admit to not having an excuse to ignore them."

Renee laughed. He seemed innocent enough. She didn't see why telling him about Gray and her quest to rekindle their love would harm anything. If anything, the man could possibly give her advice on what to say and how to approach him. Most importantly, he may be able to give her some idea of how he might react.

"Well, I'm contemplating a move from Boston back to my hometown of Greensboro."

"Really? I'm headed that way myself," he countered.

"Well, looks like we'll be flying buddies for one more flight then," Renee said, actually happy about the idea of spending another hour with the old man. He was, indeed, very sweet.

"Well, unfortunately that's not the case, dear. I have to spend a night in Atlanta. I'm not excited about it, but duty calls."

Renee frowned. "That's too bad. You're going to leave me, and chances are next flight I'll get stuck right next to one of him." She motioned over at the Armani knockoff dozed off in the seat beside him with his headphones over his ears.

He laughed. "Yeah, let's hope that isn't the case." He paused and then said, "So anyway, you are moving and…" he left the sentence unfinished.

"Yeah, I spent a little over ten years in Boston. Loved every second of it. It's such a fun town."

"So, why are you deciding to move back to Greensboro?" He smiled. "If excitement is what you're after, you're not exactly headed to a hot bed."

Renee nodded in agreement. "Trust me, I know. I'm actually not even from Greensboro, I'm from the outskirts of High Point."

"You mean Sedgefield?" he asked quickly.

"No, actually Jamestown, but they are pretty much one in the same. How do you know Sedgefield?"

"I lived in High Point nearly twenty-five years of my life, dear."

Renee realized that she and the old man had not even been formally introduced.

"You know what just occurred to me, other than my formally being Elizabeth whatever-her-last name was, we don't even know each other's names. I'm Renee Starnes." She stuck out her hand in offering.

"Douglas," he replied with a smile. He shook her hand.

She smiled back. "Well, it's nice to meet you, Douglas."

"The pleasure's all mine, Ms. Starnes."

There was a moment of awkward silence, and the two both glanced around the plane, looking at all of the other passengers who seemed to be waiting impatiently. Lost in conversation, it had somehow gone unnoticed to both of them that they had yet to take off and were only now finally approaching the runway.

"So what makes you think of leaving Boston, Renee?" Douglas finally broke the silence.

Renee turned and positioned herself back exactly as she had been before. "Hope you're ready for this one."

Denial

      Little red numbers on the digital alarm clock from the Taylor's household showed that bedtime was finally drawing near. The clock, which was the single possession Gray had brought to the hospital, was the only thing that kept him aware that there was a world outside of this room moving on at a brisk pace. His life was trapped in this little room, while his memories of what had once been a happy life were trapped inside his mind.

      At the moment, he was lost in thought. His mind focused on three completely different things: his mother, the Atlanta Braves baseball game that had finally captured his attention, and the strange old man he had met just thirty minutes earlier.

      Gray was very curious as to why he had been so chatty with the guy. He was nothing more than a mere stranger off the street, a fellow rebel in the ongoing pursuit of lung cancer. Gray wasn't the kind to entertain random conversations such as these. Maybe fifteen years earlier, but not since losing his father and sister.

He thought more about the man. Though he knew he'd never laid eyes on him, he felt as if he had met the man before. His deep blue eyes seemed so familiar, and they had the most unusual sparkle. It didn't make any sense to Gray at all, but deep in his heart, he hoped he'd run into the old man again. He seemed easy to talk to and had a peaceful, calming spirit. Gray supposed his attraction to the man was the fact that he was dealing with a very similar situation. Most likely, the old man had been dealing with his situation much longer.

He looked at Sylvia. Though he'd been watching her in this dormant condition for over a month now, he would never be able to get used to it. The way she appeared so frail and so fragile, but yet still so beautiful, made him want to break into tears. He refused to let the tears flow, however, because he knew she would soon awaken and everything would be fine. If it took him sitting by her bedside each night for the next ten years, he was prepared.

He looked up at the game again.

"Come on, Brav o's," he said to the television.

"Mike's up at the plate, Ma," he said, referring to the Braves new acquisition that was from North Carolina and who had played Little League baseball with Gray.

"Hopefully he'll come through like he did that time against Raleigh. You remember that, Mom? You were yelling so loud, I think the people in Durham could hear you."

He laughed to himself at the memory.

Sylvia Taylor was the most proud mom when it came to Gray's athletic teams, and certainly the most boisterous. She was the definitive "team mom."

"I remember I was standing on first. I had just been walked. There were two outs and we were down a run. When Mike unleashed that double and I came around to home and was ruled safe, those bleachers went into hysterics."

He continued stroking Sylvia's arm as he reminisced. "But you were the loudest, Mom. You always were."

As he finished the story, knowing that there was not going to be any response, he strongly but sadly concluded, "Those were the good times, huh Mom?"

He continued rubbing her arm as he watched the at bat. Unfortunately Mike

Norcross didn't come through, and the game went into another inning. As the commercial break began, he looked back at his mother to offer up more conversation.

"I met a really neat guy tonight, Mom. He was probably around your age. He was about my size. He had a great smile and big blue eyes. Too bad you're all laid up, he's the only man I've met that I *may* have approved of."

He laughed.

Since the death of his father and sister, Gray was not only selective, but actually intolerant of the men Sylvia attempted to date. Though it was not the manner in which he wanted his mother's dating to stop, the gentleman caller's faded away once multiple sclerosis finally forced her into a wheelchair. The wheelchair upset Gray. The demise of his mother's romantic life did not.

"Yeah, it was really strange. I just went out to smoke like I always do when Mary comes in, and he came up to ask if he could bum a smoke."

He looked down at her as if he could visualize her disapproval with the fact that the man smoked. Sylvia Taylor disliked smoking, drinking, premarital sex, and basically anything that lined up with what Christians considered sin. When her husband had picked up smoking two years before his death, she was unhappy to say the least.

"He did speak about Christianity to me, though," he said, as if he was trying to sell the man to her. "He said he'd be praying for a miracle and all that other crap." He paused. "You know, I just can't buy into all that religion, Ma. If there really is a God out there, why aren't Dad and Claire sitting here with me right now? Why are you lying here in this hospital bed at such a young age?" He looked at his mother and then sighed, "I know you don't want to hear it, but God abandoned us somewhere along the way."

He looked at her and nodded.

"But you better believe I'll never abandon you."

He stroked her arm.

"You know, I think I may have been about to tell him about the wreck."

He looked at her. He visualized the response a conscience Sylvia Taylor would have had, which would be one of utter disbelief. Gray never spoke to anyone other than Sylvia about Jack and Claire's wreck. Rarely did he even allow her to speak of it.

"He asked me about why I'd think your dying would leave me alone, and where my family was, and..." The door opened and Dr. Ravel stuck his head in.

"Hello, Mr. Taylor. How are you tonight?" The doctor attempted a genuine smile in Gray's direction, knowing it wasn't going to be reciprocated.

"I'm hanging in there," Gray returned condescendingly. He met eyes with the doctor for a second and then resumed stroking his mother.

Dr. Ravel stood quietly, debating what it was he even wanted to say. Finally, he clasped his hands together and spoke up.

"Gray, it's been over a month."

Gray had been waiting for him to break the awkward silence with a comment similar to this.

"Didn't I tell you to screw off the last time you came to me with this shit?"

"Listen, Mr. Taylor, she shows no signs of improvement. She's only stable because..."

"Do me a favor, Dr. Ravel," Gray interrupted as he motioned for the doctor to come to where he was sitting.

"Yes?" the doctor replied, confused as to what Gray wanted.

"Come on. Come over here." Again Gray motioned in his own direction.

Dr. Ravel casually strolled over to where Gray sat beside his mother's bed. "What can I do for you, Mr. Taylor."

"You're a doctor, right?"

"Yes, Mr. Taylor, I'm a doctor," he said. He was beyond fed up with the ill treatment Gray had given him the past month.

"Well do me a favor, Doc. I need you to look at something for me really quickly."

"Come again?"

"Yeah, it will only take a few seconds. Put those glasses on really quick." Gray motioned toward the seeing glasses in Dr. Ravel's right chest pocket.

"Okay, Mr. Taylor, what do you want?" he said as he slipped his glasses on his face.

"Take a look at this thing on my forehead, would ya?"

Squinting his eyes, Dr. Ravel leaned down, trying to find what it was that Gray was referring to.

"What thing, Mr. Taylor?"

"Look closer."

He looked again. "I'm sorry, but I don't see anything."

"Okay, I just needed a second opinion from someone with such an honorable degree."

"A second opinion on what?"

"That I don't in fact have a sign tattooe d to my forehead that said, 'Do you think I give a shit?'"

Dr. Ravel sighed, "Very amusing, Gray." He was tired of referring to him by the respective name, "Mr. Taylor." "Maybe one day you'll grow up."

Gray scoffed. "Well, I'll never be able to be as smart as you now, will I Dr. Ravel? Now get the hell out of here, we were talking."

Dr. Ravel stood firmly. "Gray, listen, I know this is the last thing you want to talk about. But it's my job, and you're going to listen."

Gray shot a look at him. "Unless I'm mistaken, Doc, I'm about fifteen pounds heavier than you. And though my collegiate athletic days are over, I'd venture to guess you never competed in a sport past little league - where you sat on the bench and ate ding-dongs and kept stats the whole game. Odds are I'll beat your ass, so don't tell me what I am and am not going to listen to."

"Just like a typical ex-jock that squandered all other potential he was ever blessed with: resolve everything by 'who can kick whose ass.'" Dr. Ravel sighed. "Darwin would certainly be proud."

Gray scoffed at the comment. He sat in the same position and then raised a brow that suggested Dr. Ravel go ahead and spit out that which he had come to say.

"Gray, I know you love your mother. It's apparent to everyone."

Gray didn't move a muscle. He just sat still, waiting for him to continue.

"And I really think it's a noble and loving thing you do, staying here at her bedside each day and sleeping in the room with her at night." Dr. Ravel paused, searching for the proper words.

"But there are some things you have no choice but to consider. Gray, I have been a doctor for twenty-two years now. I graduated in the top two percent of my class from Duke medical school. I have nursed literally thousands of people through cancer bouts. Some of them made a full recovery, some of them passed on."

He stopped to make sure Gray was listening. He could tell by Gray's direct eye contact that he indeed was. He continued.

"I don't give you my resume in order to brag or say I'm smarter than you, or that I'm smarter than anyone else, for that matter. I just want you to understand my credentials. I have seen situations like these many times, Gray. I speak from experience.

What I am trying to tell you is that she isn't ever going to come out of her coma. The only thing keeping her alive right now is life support. Letting her go is something you have to consider, Gray."

Gray grunted, but Dr. Ravel paid no attention.

'She's basically already gone, it's just up to you to let her go for good." He paused to let the statement sink in. "It's what she'd do for you."

Gray saw this as the chance he needed to turn the conversation back into an argument. He cocked his brow. "Oh, really? She would, would she? You think you know something about my mom?"

Dr. Ravel rolled his eyes, realizing that any civility the conversation may have once had was now lost.

"You think she'd just give up on me, huh Doc? You think she'd just give up because there didn't appear to be a chance?"

"That's not what I'm trying to s..."

"Well, let me tell you a little story, Dr. Ravel." Gray stood to his feet.

"When I was junior in college, we had a soccer tournament at Georgetown University. That weekend, my dad had to go out of town on business, and couldn't make it to see us play. My sister had plans to spend the weekend at the beach with one of her friend's families. So guess who came on her own?"

"That's wonderful Gray, and I'm sure she..." The doctor tried to interrupt, but Gray wasn't nearly finished.

"That's right. She drove all the way up on her own; six and a half-hours she drove just to be there for my tournament. She knew I wasn't going to play. She knew the coach wouldn't call me off the bench. But did that stop her from coming and sitting in the ninety degree sun, sweating her ass off?

"Yes, Gray. I understand she was a good..."

Once again, Gray didn't even let him finish a single sentence. He just kept talking.

His voice was getting stronger the deeper he got into the story.

"You want to know the most amazing thing about her coming up to D.C. that weekend, Doc; about her sitting in the hot sun while I sat on the bench?"

Dr. Ravel sighed, "What's that, Gray?"

Gray paid no attention to the tone of the doctor's voice.

"Just four days earlier the doctors had made her start taking steroids to combat her MS. What the doctors didn't know was she was allergic to those steroids. She had a temperature of one hundred and two point three. Her glands were swollen, and she had a headache that pounded like a freight train was running through her head."

As the memory of the story began flooding his mind, tears began to slowly trickle down his face.

"She sat there, in that burning hot sun. She just sat there. She was miserable. But I watched her the whole time that game went on, Doc. Never once did a smile leave her face. Not once did she get up and try to find shade to rest in. And when the coach finally did put me in with five minutes left in the game, she stood up and yelled at the top of her lungs as I ran onto the field. After the game, you would have thought that I had been the star player based on the embrace she gave me. And as our team all walked to the Metro to head back to the hotel, she didn't utter one word of complaint about how terrible she felt." He paused. "Oh, but I could see it in her eyes.

And when we stepped onto that Metro, there was one seat left. You here that? One."

He stopped to see if the doctor was following.

"My coach sat right down in that seat, not having the presence of mind to offer it to my mother or any other ladies left standing, for that matter. He just sat down and started looking over his game report. I wanted to punch him so badly right then. But right as I was about to say something, I looked over across the Metro to my mother.

With sweat trickling off her brow, her eyes shut trying to alleviate a fragment of the pain, her neck slouched and her head cocked down, she turned to where I was standing. She opened her eyes for a full second, and looked at me and forced a smile, before mouthing the words, 'I love you."

She didn't have to be there for me at that tournament, Doc. She could have easily been in bed, where ten out of ten other mothers would have been. But instead she was on that loud, crowded, Washington, D.C. Metro, with a smile on her face despite all the agony she was feeling.

So don't you stand there and tell me about your days playing croquet with all the other hotshot medical elitists. Don't you tell me what does and doesn't appear to be logical. And never, I repeat *never*, tell me what my mother would and wouldn't do for me again."

With a look that could pierce steel, he stared directly into Dr. Ravel's eyes. Tears ran down his cheeks.

"I will not let go of my mother, Dr. Ravel. Not for you, not for anybody."

Dr. Ravel sighed. Sympathetically he replied, "I'm sorry to hear that, Gray."

Dr. Ravel turned, opened the door, and headed back down the hallway to pack up his things to head home.

Gray stood still for a moment, and the remainder of the tears he had tried to hide now shed at the rate they wanted to from the beginning of the story. He turned and sat back down in his chair. He grabbed Sylvia's hand and through muffled tears he said, "I'll never let you go, Mom. Never."

A Reason for Leaving

The captain had finally turned on "the fasten seat belt" sign and had reported that Delta Flight 443 was to be landing at the Piedmont Triad International Airport in eight minutes. Renee rubbed her temples, attempting to alleviate the headache that came compliments of a full day of flying and layovers.

The flight had been fine. It was only a forty-five minute hop, skip, and jump from Atlanta to Greensboro, and she had napped for about twenty of it. She had been ticketed in a window seat as she would have preferred on the previous flight but had found herself wishing she could meet someone else as interesting as Doug had been from New York to Atlanta.

The flight with Douglas, whom she later asked if it was kosher to call "Doug," was indeed pleasant. He was a kind, gentle old man, who was very charming and had an exceptional listening ear.

Renee spent most of the flight telling him about Gray and her reasons for coming back to see him. By the end of the flight, he had given her his assurance that Gray would be sympathetic to her plea for forgiveness. Though he was just a stranger, his opinion gave Renee the confidence she needed to confront Gray.

She also told him all about how she moved in with one of the senior partners from her firm, Alex Delaney, and how the two talked of marriage numerous times. She explained that though she always felt Alex was a wonderful, brilliant man, she never experienced the excitement as she did when she was with Gray. She claimed this to be the reason she could never go through with a marriage to Delaney. It just wasn't quite true love. She did giggle a bit when she admitted that the sex was still great.

Finally, the plane started dropping and then climaxed with screeching wheels on the hard asphalt runway. Home sweet home. Renee sighed. She looked out the window of the plane, trying to get her first glimpse of her hometown in over four years, but the dark fog that covered the night sky was too thick. She smiled and laughed to herself. Inside she found herself saying, "Well, Renee, here we go. Here's to a new life."

She stood and gathered her belongings. Finally, she filed out of the plane with the rest of the crowd, and headed to the baggage claim where she would fall into the open arms of her mother.

Confronting The Past

Gray awoke restlessly to the familiar, uncomfortable feeling of sleeping in a wooden hospital chair. He grabbed at the arms of the chair and thrust his weight in one direction and then in the other, attempting to pop his back. His back popped successfully, and he reached his arms in the air, yawning as he stretched.

He had been sleeping in the hospital room every night since his mother had fallen into her coma. It was an uncomfortable situation, but the thought of leaving his mother by herself overnight had never even crossed his mind. He must be there when she woke up- or, curse God if it were to happen, when she finally breathed her last.

He stood from his chair and gently folded his blanket and tucked it away in the closet behind him. He walked over to Sylvia's bed, leaned over, gave her a kiss, and said, "Morning, Mama."

He smiled at her for a second, and then proceeded to tell her what his plans were. He glanced at his watch. "It's going on 9:15, Mom. I'm gonna go down and grab some coffee. I'll be back to see ya here in a few." He watched her lie there for a moment, before turning to head for the elevator.

As he hopped in, he was pleased to find that he was the only person occupying the downward climb. He hated being stuck aboard the elevator with people in mid- conversation.

The elevator continued its descent from Gray's sixth floor starting point, all the way to the second floor. Suddenly, it came to a stop with a loud "ding," and the doors waited patiently as they prepared to open. Gray cringed but knew he only had to ride with whomever it was for a single story. He just hoped they wouldn't attempt idle conversation. He was too tired to pretend to feign interest.

As the doors gave way, Gray was overcome with delight to see Mary walk in to join him.

"Good morning, Mary," he said, offering a smile. The pretty face had quickly changed his mood.

"Well, hello, Gray," she said, flashing her million-dollar grin. "Where you headed?"

"Coffee time."

"Me too," she replied. "In the cafeteria?"

"Yeah. It ain't Starbucks- but it's free."

"You can say that again. Who can afford to pay five dollars for a cappuccino?"

"I'm sure Dr. Ravel wouldn't have a problem with it. He finished in the top two percent of his class at Duke Med.," Gray replied mockingly.

Mary laughed. "He's actually a really good guy, Gray. You really oughta give him a chance."

Gray frowned. "I suppose I go a little rough on him. But he *is* basically asking me to kill my mother. Not a good way to start a relationship."

Mary was about to attempt a reply, but the elevator dinged again, signaling they had reached their destination. Mary was thankful because she was not prepared to give a tactful response.

"Shall we?" Gray asked generically, as he motioned for the lady to exit before him.

"Indeed," she said with a coy smile.

The two walked from the elevator, past the lobby area, and into the cafeteria.

"What can I get for you, oh wise woman of medicine?" Gray asked, walking toward the coffee station in the corner.

"Oh God, don't- you make me feel like Jane Seymour!" She laughed at her joke.

"What? Who is that?"

"You know, Jane Seymour. She played Dr. Quinn the Medicine Woman. You remember that awful show, don't you?'

"Unfortunately, yes. But I had luckily not been forced to think of it until this very moment."

Mary laughed.

'Seriously, though, all bad 90's television shows aside, what can I get you?" he asked again.

"Decaf- two creams, one sugar."

"Decaf? I'll never understand the point," he said. He smiled and turned to get their morning stimulants.

He poured Mary's cup of decaf, two creams and one sugar, just like she had asked, and then he tilted it and took a sip.

"Yep, as weak as I thought," he whispered to himself.

He then poured his coffee, which he was pleased to see was freshly brewed, and then added a cream and a sugar.

He placed stir straws in each, picked them both up, and walked over to where Mary sat waiting at a table for two.

"Thank you, kind sir," she said, as he handed her the decaffeinated creation.

"Don't mention it." He took a sip. "Ah, nothing like a cup of hospital coffee to get your day started off on the wrong foot," he said sarcastically.

"Oh don't complain about getting your day started young man. I've been up and moving around this hospital since 7:15."

"Well they certainly have you putting in your hours, now don't they? You were here last night until nearly 9:00."

"9:30 to be exact," she replied.

"Why are they working you so hard?"

She shrugged. "I guess because I'm new here."

Gray took another sip. "How long did you say you've been here, again?"

"Just over a month. Remember, your mom was my first patient."

"Oh yeah. No wonder you take such good care of her," he said. He offered her a heartfelt smile.

"Yeah, she seems like a very special lady."

Gray nodded.

"She must be special, to have a son like you who sits by her bedside day and night."

Gray slowly sipped his coffee and then shrugged. "Trust me, she's special. If I were the one in that hospital bed, she'd not only be sitting at my bedside day and night, she'd be reading books on how to be a doctor herself."

Mary laughed. "You guys must have been awfully close."

"Close doesn't come anywhere in the vicinity of describing it, babe," he said as he held up his pack of Marlboro's, questioning whether she minded his lighting up. She shook her head no.

Gray removed a single cigarette from the pack and put it to his lips. He lit it and inhaled.

"You see, it's been just us for over ten years now."

"What do you mean, 'just us?' Where's your father or your brother's and sisters?"

She paused.

"What about your friends?" Isn't there anyone else you're close to?"

Gray took a deep drag and exhaled. He couldn't believe how similar Mary's question was to the one the old man had asked him the night before. Strangely, he felt fully prepared to give Mary a detailed answer. He wondered why he was all of a sudden feeling so comfortable with the idea of sharing Jack and Claire's misfortune.

"Yeah, I've got friends," he began through the recently exhaled smoke. "At least, I guess you could say that. I haven't really seen or spoken to any of them in years." He took another drag.

"Well, why is that, Gray?"

He shrugged. "I guess because after the accident and the break up, I didn't feel like those relationships were important anymore. I didn't feel like anyone was really there for me- except, of course, for my mom."

Mary leaned closer. She searched him with prying eyes. "What wreck and break up, Gray?"

Gray leaned back in his chair, attempting to get comfortable.

"Well, it was late December of 2000. I was fresh off of graduation, and I had moved back home from my college in Virginia to write for the <u>Enterprise</u>. You know, our local paper here."

She nodded, indicating she was familiar with the <u>High Point Enterprise</u>.

"Well I wasn't completely excited about living in High Point again." He laughed sarcastically. "Not exactly the most exciting place in the world for a twenty-two year old kid, ya know?"

She smiled.

"Well, I was working late one night, wrapping up a deadline for the next morning. I was the only staff member left in the office. Suddenly, my phone rang. I went to answer it, expecting it to be my fiancée, Renee, calling to see why she wasn't able to reach me at my apartment. I answered the phone, and all I could hear was hysterical crying."

Mary observed that Gray's eyes were staring passed her as he talked, as if he were remembering the entire situation like it was yesterday.

"It was my mom, calling to tell me that my father and sister had been in a car accident."

Mary reached her hand out to grab Gray's, "Oh, Gray. I'm sor…"

He kept talking right above her. His emotional instability indicated that he had been waiting to audibly tell the story for years.

"I, at first, tried to be calm. I started asking things like, 'How are they? Are they okay? Are they in the hospital?' Saying things like, 'Mom, get a hold of yourself. Where are they?'"

Tears started dropping from his eyes.

'She said. 'They're gone Gray. They're gone. They're gone to be with Jesus.'"

He paused for nearly ten seconds, as he sat remembering the entire event. Finally, he wiped the tears from his face.

"I lost it, Mary. I absolutely lost it. I started screaming in the phone. Screaming things like, 'Don't you tell me that. Don't you dare tell me that!' I didn't even cry for the first few seconds; I was too enraged. I was too mad at whoever hit them; too mad at God. To be honest, I didn't even know who I was mad at. I finally started crying with her. She just kept telling me how much she loved me and how we were going to fight through it together. I couldn't even speak, Mary. I couldn't offer her a single word of encouragement. I wasn't strong enough." He stopped, as if thinking for a second. Finally, he sighed. "I'll never be strong enough."

"Finally, I told her I'd be over in a few minutes."

Mary watched him as he continued to speak, but she didn't offer up a single word of reply. Instead, she just sat listening intently, not wanting to break his concentration.

"I hopped in my car and drove like the wind. I hadn't even asked where the wreck was or even what had caused it, for that matter. I had no idea why I had just lost my father and sister; all I knew was that my life would never be the same.

When I got to my parent's house, my mom was waiting for me on the porch. She was bundled up on the front steps with nothing but a blanket. She looked up to me as I ran up the stone walkway to our front door."

Gray sat quietly. Mary could tell he was fighting back more tears. He spoke softly.

"Tears streamed down her face, Mary. Her mascara ran from her eyes and covered her cheeks. As I neared her, she stood to her feet and opened her arms, inviting me to come inside her blanket. As I fell into her, she just kept saying, 'I love you, Gray. I love you so much.'"

Gray just kept whispering these last words, and Mary realized he was so lost in memory that he had forgotten he was even talking to someone. Finally he snapped out of it.

"Anyway, we went inside the house. I asked her what had happened. She had finally settled down a bit and was ready to tell me the story. We sat together on the living room couch. She told me that it had, in legalistic terms, been my father's fault. He had attempted to make a left-hand turn across a four-way intersection, without having the green arrow to turn. He was hit by a large Ford- F150 right in Claire's passenger door."

Mary grimaced.

"Here's the thing though, Mary. Yeah, it was my dad's fault. But the truth of the matter was, the guy who hit them had more than enough time to see them and stop. But the guy was coming from Big Jim's tavern and had just blown a tab of forty- seven fifty on Budweiser's and shots of Jack Daniels. He was hammered."

Mary looked at him sympathetically.

"You see, at that intersection, if you're coming straight through the light, you have a good one hundred yards to see if there is any traffic ahead. He was so drunk, that he didn't even take note of the car that had pulled right out in front of him. The accident report didn't show a single sign of a breaking attempt on his part."

Gray stopped to let the whole story sink in.

"For the life of me, Mary, I don't know why my dad was turning through that intersection. My best guess is that Claire had kept messing with the radio like she always did, and maybe my dad was sick of listening to her punk rock music. Maybe he was changing the channel, putting in a CD of his own. But whatever the case, I lost my father and sister that night, and it wasn't on account of a traffic error by my father. Instead, it was due to the disregard of an alcoholic." He sighed. "And that's why there's no dad or sibling to speak of."

He sat back in his chair, and reached for the ashtray to kill the flare of his finished cigarette. Mary continued to sit quietly, not knowing what to say or whether Gray was even finished. Finally, seeing that he had completed as much of the story as he wished to tell, she asked, "Well the guy's at least rotting in prison, right?"

Gray chuckled sarcastically.

"Oh, Mary, Mary, quite contrary, how does your garden grow?"

He laughed again.

"So naïve we are." He grabbed another cigarette from his pack and lit up.

"Our United States legal system is indeed that: *legal*, not logical." Mockingly, he laughed again.

"A finely hand-picked jury by the defense attorney of one Tanner Buckman ruled that my father was at fault for the accident, and that good ol' Tanner only had to spend six months in an alcohol rehabilitation center."

"Well that doesn't seem fair," Mary responded quickly.

Gray laughed at the comment. "Yeah, I kinda had those same feelings myself." He puffed on his cigarette. "I'm not saying that's how the court's going to rule on a case exactly like that one, every single time." He exhaled. "But do you know what the color of justice is in this country, Mary Thorn?"

"What's that, Gray?"

"Green; deep, emerald green. And it comes with a bold saying tattooed on it. And you know what that is?"

Mary shrugged. "What?"

"In God We Trust," Gray said. He snickered. "Here's to you up there, big guy," He mockingly tipped his coffee in toast.

Mary wanted desperately to defend her belief in God but felt it to be completely the wrong time to do so. She offered a hesitant smile instead.

Gray finished the sip and took another drag from his cigarette before finally concluding the topic with, 'So your guess is as good as mine as to where he is right now. But yes, I certainly hope he's rotting."

Mary wanted to ask him what he was referring to earlier about his break up, but she assumed it was in regards to the fiancée he had mentioned before, and she felt that since Gray had already dealt with one deep issue today, she shouldn't push the envelope. This was the first time since Sylvia had been in the hospital that he had shown any sign of opening up to her. Also, she had to go check on Sylvia.

She looked at Gray and said, "Well, I'm truly sorry to hear all that, Gray. I'm sure that must have been extremely rough. I'm sure you and your sister were probably just as close as you and your mother are."

He just nodded. " We were best friends, Mary. Even though we were fully grown she had never stopped calling me, 'Bubby.'"

"Bubby?"

Gray chuckled. "Yeah, when she was first learning how to talk, she couldn't say 'Brother,' so Bubby is what I became."

Mary smiled. "Well I'm sure she misses you too, Gray."

Gray smiled at the thought and then sighed. "I'm sorry to have dumped all of that on you. I know none of that is your concern."

She smiled. "Of course it's my concern, Gray. I care a great deal for you. It was a pleasure to listen."

It was a major source of comfort for Gray to hear that Mary cared for him.

"You know, you're the first person I've ever told that story to, Mary. I rarely even spoke of it with Mom."

"Really?"

He shook his head.

"So then, why me, Gray? What made you want to tell me?"

Gray shrugged, realizing he had no answer to the question. "I really don't know, Mary. I feel strangely close to you. You've been good to my mother. Plus, you're a real person. You're genuine. There are very few genuine people left in this world."

She nodded in agreement. She was about to say "thanks" and remove herself from the conversation, but he kept talking.

"It also might have something to do with my finally feeling the need to confront some things."

She had begun to stand, but as he spoke, she sat back down.

"Yeah, it's really strange, because it wasn't until last night that I had felt any inclination to speak about our past."

"Well, what was special about last night?" she questioned.

"I'm not sure anything especially," he said. "I met that guy I told you about last night. You know, that Rose guy. It was weird. He asked me a few questions, and for some reason, I didn't feel the bitterness I always have before. I didn't really have any reservations."

"Do you have any idea why?" Mary asked.

Gray shrugged. "I don't really know. He seemed like a genuine person too." He sighed. "Maybe I have just needed the right type of people to listen."

"Well, I'm glad to have been the one you shared that with, Gray. It's an honor. You know how close I feel to your mother."

"Yes, I do, Mary, and I can never tell you how much it means to me."

Mary smiled. "It's my pleasure, Gray. But I have to be going now; I have to go see how our girl's doing."

"Okay, I'll see ya later this afternoon. Again, thanks for listening."

"Anytime."

Mary turned and walked back in the direction of the elevator. Gray reached for the newspaper that had been left at the table beside him. He opened up the sports page, lit up a cigarette, and began reading about the upcoming Major League Baseball strike.

"*Damn overpaid bunch of crybabies,*" he said to himself, as he inhaled his cigarette and settled into the article.

An Invitation

"How's the day going, Merle?" Gray asked the elderly black lady as he walked past her toward the door.

"Can't complain. My grandbaby won a spelling bee at his school yesterday."

"Good for him. Have a good one."

"You too, Mr. Taylor. I do wish you'd find you a woman out there."

"Don't see that happening, Merle. I'll see ya later."

Gray walked through the double doors and out into the cold January afternoon. He had spent about thirty more minutes in the cafeteria after Mary had left, reading the paper and occupying time. He then went back up and sat with Sylvia and talked to her about having recounted the story of the wreck. Finally, 12:30 had come around, and it was time for him to make his daily trip to the local deli.

The deli was only about four blocks from the hospital, and Gray felt it to be a very convenient distance. It wasn't too far to have to drive, yet it was far enough for him to get a bit of exercise. He zipped his coat and prepared for the trek.

He'd been coming to the deli everyday since Sylvia had been in the hospital. He knew all of the employees by name and had the cost value of his favorite sandwich down to a science.

He always walked to the store with the hope that Gerald, his favorite sandwich artist, would be working. Gerald was a man twenty years or so Gray's elder and, Gray observed, was not working the job because it was something to occupy his time. Likely, he needed the money, and it was the only job he could get.

Gerald was a precious, little old man with Gray hair, wrinkles, and glasses that sat on the edge of his nose as he made his sandwiches. Gerald was one of those special few that always had a smile on his face. Each day Gray would watch as spoiled, rich teenagers would come in and order their sandwiches with attitudes that suggested that they were "better" than Gerald . Meanwhile, Gerald never let the smile fade from his face.

He just kept asking what they'd like on their sandwich, would prepare it, ring them up, and then wish them a good day and genuinely offer the standard fast food service goodbye: "Please, come back and see us again soon."

Gray continued walking, passing the *Krispy Kreme* donut shop and the *Nation's Bank* on his left. He stared across the street at the old, abandoned fire station and the overpriced hair boutique. High Point was indeed a quaint little town. It was quaint, quiet, and slow-moving: the perfect recipe for the hermit Gray had become.

Finally he arrived at the sandwich shop, and opened the door to enter. He cringed at the sound of the entry bells that hung on the door. He had always found their ring to be such an obnoxious noise.

"How are you today, Mr. Taylor?" Gerald asked as he saw Gray walk in.

"I'm hanging in there. How are you, Gerald?"

"Can't complain."

"Let me guess, club sandwich, plain, add light mustard."

"You know me too well, Gerald." Gray smiled.

"One boring sandwich with a little yellow seasoning, coming right up," Gerald chided.

"Hey, at least it's easy for you to make, Gerald."

"You can say that again, Mr. Taylor."

Gray smiled at him. He hated being called Mr. Taylor by people older than he was. It was a sign of disrespect to have to call someone your minor by his surname.

'So how's that mother of yours doing, Mr. Taylor?" Gerald asked, as he took turns applying the different meats included in the sandwich.

'Same ol,' same ol' unfortunately, Gerald, but thanks for asking."

Gerald looked up and smiled, but didn't say anything more. Gray was thankful for the fact that there was one person who didn't feel the need to say that they'd be praying for her. At least the whole town hadn't been brainwashed.

"Well, that will be..." he attempted to tell Gray the cost of his meal, but Gray finished it for him.

"$7.97. Come on, Gerald, you think you're speaking to a novice?"

Gerald smiled back reluctantly, and Gray assumed he just didn't know what the word "novice" meant.

"You have a good day, Mr. Taylor." He handed Gray his change.

"You too, Gerald."

Gray took his food and headed to the table nestled away in the back corner of the dining area. He sat in the same spot everyday. Its location allowed him to observe all others who came in and out of the shop, but at the same time, kept him far enough removed to avoid any conversation.

"$7.97," he whispered to himself as he unwrapped the sandwich. "I remember when it used to be $5.34 back in college." He grabbed the sandwich and took a bite.

He lifted his head as he heard the sound of the obnoxious jingle at the front of the store. He was shocked when he saw Colonel Rose standing in the doorway.

"Hey, Colonel Rose," he yelled from his spot in the corner.

"Taylor, how are ya, ol' boy?" The old man flashed him a smile as he walked to where Gerald stood braced to prepare his sandwich. The Colonel stuck a finger in the air, motioning he'd be over to sit with Gray as soon as he ordered his food.

Gray nodded back in acceptance.

"Keep the change," the Colonel said as Gerald attempted to hand him his leftover sixty- two cents.

"I'm sorry, Sir, we're not allowed to accept tips."

"Well, then put it in that penny jar there. Maybe someone can buy a cookie with it or something."

"Sure thing, Sir. Have a nice day, and please, come back to see us again soon."

Gray smiled as he heard the familiar words trickle off Gerald's lips.

"Taylor, Taylor, Taylor," the Colonel said as he walked up to Gray's table. "How are ya, kid?"

"I'm alive," Gray responded.

"That's not as easy an accomplishment as some might think," the old man said with a smile. He sat down and spread his food across the table. "So, what have you been doing today, Gray?"

"Oh, just the everyday. I had some coffee and talked to Mom for awhile. Then I walked over here and started eating. Nothing exciting."

"You kidding me? I'm on the edge of my seat waiting for more details." The Colonel laughed.

"Well, laugh all you want, but I actually did do something new today," Gray said.

"Well now, really?" the Colonel perked up.

"Yeah, I ran into one of the nurses from the hospital on my way down for my coffee this morning. I ended up sitting and talking with her for about thirty minutes."

"Well, congratulations; you flirted with a nurse!" He shook his head. "To think I really was expecting some entertainment."

"Very funny, old man. But seriously, we sat and talked for a long time. And the reason that today is any different than any other day is that I told her a story I haven't spoken of for over a decade."

The Colonel shifted in his seat. "Well, now, she must have been one good-looking nurse to get you to come out with something like that."

Gray laughed. "Well, she is very attractive. But I don't think that's what made me tell her the story."

"Well, whatever the case, I'm glad to hear that, son. What's this nurse's name?"

"Mary Thorn," Gray said. He took a sip of his soft drink.

"Well, why didn't you tell me you were talking about Mary, Taylor?"

"You know Mary?"

"You bet. First day my wife was checked in to the hospital I met her. I struck up a conversation with her. She said it was her first day on the job. I haven't seen her since, though. I'll tell you one thing that's for sure, that girl is a real peach- I guarantee the apple of some daddy's eye."

"Yeah, she's a looker all right," Gray said. "But that's strange, I asked her if she knew either you or your wife, and she said no."

The Colonel thought about it for a second. "Well, like I said, I only met her once, and it was her first day. Plus, keep in mind, we meet only a handful of nurses, they probably meet a thousand people a day."

"Good point."

"So what are you're plans for tonight?" the Colonel asked, changing subjects. "Going out with one of your lady friends?"

Gray laughed sarcastically. "Colonel, I haven't had a lady friend in ten years."

The Colonel sat back in his chair. "God, son, are you gay?"

"No, heavens no," Gray said, scoffing at the thought. "Nothing against gays, but I just can't see myself swinging that way."

"Well, then what's the problem, kid? A good looking boy like you- shoot, I'd think the girls would be climbing all over you."

Gray laughed. "Well, there was a time when I considered myself to be good with the ladies. But I have pretty much isolated myself for the past ten years or so."

"And why on earth would you do that?"

"Well, it's funny you should ask. That's another one of those stories I never speak of."

"Well, do tell, Taylor, I'm all ears." He took a bite of his sandwich.

"Well, you see, I lost my father and sister in a drunk driving accident when I was twenty-two."

The Colonel cringed. "Rough."

Gray nodded. "Indeed." He took a bite of his own sandwich. "But that's a whole other story I've already exhausted myself on for the day."

"Understandable," the Colonel replied.

Gray fixed his eyes on the old man. "How would you like to hear about Renee?"

"Renee?" the Colonel asked.

"Yep, Renee." Gray paused. "My ex-fiancée."

The Colonel took a sip of his drink and sat straight up, giving Gray his undivided attention.

"Oh, this one's gonna be good."

Gray popped his knuckles.

"Renee and I dated all through high school. We were what people call 'high school sweethearts.' I graduated a year before her and went off to college in Virginia to play soccer. She graduated the following year and decided she wanted to stay in North Carolina, so she headed to Chapel Hill, where she enrolled in their pre-law program. The distance was tough, but we made it work. The summer directly following my graduation, I proposed. We set a wedding date for the next summer. Things were great. She was planning to move to Boston to attend law school, and I had been shown some interest from the Boston Globe- which was more than enough to get me excited about accompanying her to Bean town."

Gray stopped for a moment and took a bite of his sandwich. He washed it down with his cola. The Colonel just sat quietly in waiting.

"That year I was living in High Point, writing for the <u>Enterprise</u> as I was waiting for her to graduate from UNC. One night, I was working late, and I got a call from my mom, announcing that my father and sister had died in the car wreck I just told you about."

The Colonel frowned and nodded, indicating he was following along with the timeline of the story.

"So after heading home to console my mother, I gave Renee a call to tell her the bad news."

Gray took another sip.

"She was very sympathetic. She cried with me on the phone for a long time. She was extremely close to both of them. But, anyway, as the conversation went on, I told her that I had been forced to make a decision. Renee knew full well that my mother had multiple sclerosis, which was all but promising to put her in a wheelchair in the next three to five years. She also knew full well that nothing meant more to me than my mother. So I told her that I was not going to be able to move to Boston with her because I was going to have to move back in with my mom. I told her that if she truly loved me, she'd put her career plans aside, and we'd all live together in High Point."

Gray sighed remembering the conversation.

"So anyway, I suppose telling you her response isn't necessary because I'm sitting here by myself today."

The Colonel sat still for a moment. "Man, that's a tough break, kid."

"Yep," Gray said, taking the last bite of his club.

"So, why'd ya take yourself out of the game for good?"

Gray shrugged. "Don't really have an exact answer, Colonel. I guess it's a mixture of being bitter toward Renee for leaving me, bitter toward God for stealing my family, and the knowledge that the only thing I could ever really count on in the world was my mom. So after all of that, I began distancing myself from everything else, and simply comforting myself in my relationship with Mom. Which brings us to the present. So here we are, Colonel. Here's to you and me."

Gray raised his cup in the air.

"To what could be my best conscious friend in the world." He chuckled as he mocked his plight.

"Anyway, thanks for listening. Getting this shit off my chest really does feel good. I probably should have done this years ago."

The Colonel smiled. "No problem, kid. I tell ya what. Seeing as I've recently become your new best friend, why don't we have dinner tonight?"

Gray sat back and thought for a moment. "Thanks, but I can't leave Mom alone for that long, I..."

The Colonel cut him off.

"She'll be fine, Gray. It'l l only be for a couple hours. Besides, I bet if you asked her, Mary would promise to keep a very careful watch on her." He smiled, knowing the mention of Mary would excite Gray.

Gray was very timid about the idea.

"I don't know. I haven't left her alone for that long before."

"Oh, come on, Gray; there's nothing wrong with living a little."

Gray thought again. Hesitantly he said, "Well I suppose I could go out for a little while."

The Colonel smiled. "Great, then we're on. Meet me at just before seven."

Gray glanced at his watch. That was in five hours. He'd actually have to go home and shower.

"Okay, that sounds good. Where do you want to go?"

The Colonel scratched his chin as he pondered all of the local restaurants. "Well, I'm in the mood for a good meal tonight. How's the Village Tavern sound to you?"

Gray frowned. "I don't know, Colonel. That's where I proposed to Renee. I don't think I'm ready to head back there anytime soon."

"Oh come on, kid, get over it. You said yourself that was over ten years ago. Besides, it's not like her ghost is going to be there or anything."

Gray snickered. "I suppose you're right."

"Of course I'm right." The Colonel laughed. "And if we're going to be best friends, you better get used to that."

Gray laughed and then sat back in his seat. Meanwhile, the Colonel shoved the last bite of his sandwich into his mouth.

"Well, I have to be running, Taylor. I have to look in on my wife really quickly and then get some things done. I'll see you tonight around seven."

"Okay, I'll see ya then," Gray said as the Colonel stood to leave.

The Colonel walked over to the trash can and emptied his tray of leftover wrappers and his empty cup. He walked out the front door to the sound of jingling. Gray sat back and sipped on his drink. He thought about how odd it was going to feel to actually get out of the hospital. Truthfully, he was very excited.

A Bitter Rejection

Gray sat in his usual chair beside Sylvia's bed. He replayed the day's events through his head and realized he had strayed far from his comfort zone. In less than four hours, he had revealed two stories that had been bottled inside for years. He had spoken of events he never even allowed Sylvia to discuss. He couldn't figure out why, but changes were suddenly taking place in his life. And he felt better- he felt much better. He took Sylvia's hand in his, as he always did while he'd sit by her bed.

"Mom, you'll never believe what happened today." He forced a smile.

"I had coffee with Mary this morning, and I told her about dad and Claire's accident." He continued rubbing her hand. "She is such an amazing person, Mom."

He ran his fingers through her hair, and then tucked the strands back behind her ear.

"And then I went to get a sandwich for lunch, and guess who happened to be getting a sub at the exact same time? It was the guy I told you about last night, Colonel Rose.

He and I sat and ate together, and before I knew it, I found myself telling him all about Renee. I told him about our break up and how much it hurt me."

He paused and then sighed. "I really wish you could meet this guy, mom."

Even though he knew Sylvia couldn't hear a word he was saying, it felt good to acknowledge that some form of happiness had crept into his life. Though discussing both of these tragic events had taken a great deal out of him, Gray felt as if a large burden had been removed. Most importantly, he experienced the feeling that there were some people other than Sylvia who actually cared about him, and that's what really felt good.

Just then, he heard a knock at the door. Surprised, he stood to answer it. As he walked to the door, he wondered who it might be. Mary never knocked when coming in, and though Dr. Ravel normally did, it was a courtesy knock just before entering the room.

As he opened the door, he couldn't believe his eyes. A million thoughts rushed to his head at once, and not a single one settled in time to help him get a grip on the situation. He stood dumbfounded.

"Hello, Gray." Renee stood before him, staring at him with hopeful eyes. He could sense she too felt awkward.

"Renee?" Gray still couldn't believe she was standing before him.

Renee nodded her head, and stepped closer to give him a hug.

Gray let her in for a half second before backing away.

"What are you doing here, Renee?"

Renee could sense that not only was he not happy to see her, but he was in fact angry. This was the response she had been scared of until having spoken with Douglas on the airplane. Douglas had been so confident that Gray would hear her out and simply forgive her. As she studied the bitterness in Gray's eyes, she realized she had been right all along. She got defensive.

"Well, uh, Mom told me where I could find you..."

Gray cut her off.

"How did she know? Hardly anyone knows about Mom." He felt his blood boiling.

"Dr. Stansbury told Marilyn, and she told my mom at Bridge Club. I- I didn't mean to intrude."

Gray spoke quickly. "Well that's exactly what you're doing. You can't just waltz back into my life and simply say 'hi.' – You can't expect for me to pretend things between you and me are just dandy. I mean, look behind me Renee. My mom is dying. Dying!"

Renee didn't know exactly what to say. "I- I'm sorry, Gray."

Gray chuckled. 'Sorry? You're 'sorry?' You see, she's about to leave me, Renee. But you want to know the difference between you and my mother? She doesn't have a choice."

For the first time, she witnessed the severity of how deeply she had hurt him years ago. She knew he was right to be angry, and she didn't know what else to say. Had she been able to find her composure, she would have certainly opted to follow his statement with something different than what indeed came out. But instead she replied, "I still love you, Gray."

Gray couldn't believe the words he had just heard. In all honesty, they felt good. They felt really good. But he would not allow himself to acknowledge that. He laughed at her.

"You still love me, huh?"

Renee nodded her head. "Yes, Gray. I always have." She paused. "And I always will."

Gray looked her sternly in the eyes for about five seconds. He knew she was being truthful. Finally, he spoke up.

"Well, Renee, when you walked out of my life ten years ago, the door shut behind you. Now, it's locked. It's locked, and I threw away the key a long time ago. So unless you have something to say to my mother, I think you best be on your way. I am spending what little time is left with the woman who never had to provide me lip service about loving me forever."

He paused. "Please, tell your mother I said 'hi.'"

"But, Gray..." Renee tried to get in a final word.

"Leave, Renee. I mean it. Thank you for coming by, but please leave."

Renee didn't know what to do. Inside, she felt her world collapsing. Gently, she reached out her hand and touched his arm. "I'm sorry you feel that way, Gray." She turned and exited the room just as quickly as she had entered it.

Gray closed the door behind her and then walked back to his mother.

"Can you believe that just happened, Mom? The audacity of that girl..."

Inside, he felt a tugging at his heart. What was happening in his life?

Pandora's Box

The rusty hinges of the frame creaked as Gray pushed the door open. He flicked on the light and marveled at the home's state of disarray. This was, indeed, the first time he'd been home in weeks.

Though convicted by a slight feeling of betrayal, along with some nervous jitters about actually going out for an evening, Gray was excited. This was the first dinner offer in over three years that he had not declined.

He flicked on a few more lights to ensure his ability to make it to the staircase without falling and then proceeded to climb the stairs en route to the bathroom. However, before making it to the bathroom, he stopped himself just outside the doorway to his room. He stood in the doorway for nearly a full minute, replaying the dialogue between him and Renee. He tried desperately to rationalize his crude behavior and realized that he could lie to everyone in the world about no longer caring for Renee. However, he didn't know if he could ever con himself into believing that farce.

He was confused. More confused than ever, actually. How could she walk right back into his life? Just like that? No warning? No heads up?--- No nothing? Did she even have the right? He needed answers. He needed to know how he was supposed to feel because, though he had been stern in the altercation, his heart had melted the moment he had laid eyes on her.

He flicked on the light to his room and walked over to the desk in the corner. Judging by the vast amount of scattered papers atop it, one would be inclined to believe he had done a lot of work here just before Sylvia was moved to the hospital. The truth of the matter, however, was that he had barely even touched the desk since the night of Jack and Claire's wreck. To Gray, the desk was filled with too many old memories, and being near it was like opening Pandora's box.

He stared at the top right drawer for a good three minutes before finally pulling it open. This was the drawer whose contents haunted Gray daily.

The first thing he grabbed as he reached into the drawer was the beginning of the untitled novel he had begun writing in college. It was intended to be a novel about his love and admiration for Sylvia. As soon as Jack and Claire had been killed, the book's biblical premise had died along with them. Hence, the novel was cast aside.

He held the papers for a second and then dropped them on the desk before reaching back inside. The next object he retrieved was exactly what he was looking for. It was a simple scrapbook.

As he brought the scrapbook out of the drawer, he lifted it to his face and blew off the dust that covered its binding. As the dust blew away, the words "Gray and Renee" were revealed in gold lettering on the cover. It had been a Christmas present she had given him his senior year at William and Mary.

His hands trembled as he opened it.

On the first page was a picture of the two of them. Gray remembered the picture like it was yesterday. It was taken in Renee's living room, just before Gray's high school prom. Underneath it, Renee had written:

"Gray Leighton Taylor & Meredith Renee Starnes, September 24, 1995- 'Til Death Do Us Part."

A million memories rushed to Gray's head as he stared at the photograph. The night the picture was snapped was the night he had become a man. It was the night he had lost his virginity. Most importantly, however, it was the night he knew beyond a shadow of a doubt that he was in love. Quickly, he flipped to the next page.

This page revealed more pictures, more sentimental memories that had been blocked and hidden away for years. He flipped again. And then again. And again. Each page brought the same result: more and more fond memories of what once was.

Finally, he came to the last page and stared at the last remaining piece of evidence of their relationship: the letter he wrote her just after she moved to Boston.

The letter had begged her to come home. It held his confession of undying love for her. In the letter, he had told her that he couldn't live a happy life without her. It was the summation of their love. It was the perfect letter.

Before sealing it, Gray had thought long and hard about everything the letter entailed.

All of a sudden, the reality of the situation finally dawned on him. Renee had left him. She had left him, and she was not coming back. His final romantic fantasy about the inherent goodness of life flickered away, and he closed the gateway to his heart. After that night, bitterness was all that would remain.

    As Gray stood reading the letter, every single feeling from that moment ten years ago encapsulated him again. As he had looked at the old pictures and all of the other memorabilia in the scrapbook, he had felt himself vulnerable for the first time in a decade. He knew he was being wooed by the hope of love.
    But as he read that final letter, he remembered why he had opted to close the book on their relationship. This letter was all the proof he needed. He decided that he had, indeed, made the right decision in his confrontation with Renee that afternoon. Love had turned its back on him long ago, and he would, therefore, forever keep his back turned on it.

In his mind, the day Sylvia finally breathed her last, was the day in which no more love would remain in him.

Having garnered the confirmation he needed, he closed the scrapbook, dropped it back in the drawer, and placed the beginning of his old novel atop it. He pushed the drawer shut. As he walked out of his room and headed toward the bathroom, he told himself the conversation with Renee that afternoon no longer had to bother him. He'd just shower and go meet the Colonel.

Again, he realized he could lie to everyone- everyone but himself.

A Feeling of Betrayal

Gray sat quietly beside Sylvia's bed. He was freshly shaved and combed, and he was clothed in Polo Chinos and a white button-down shirt. The cologne he wore reminded him of a time when problems were a distant thought. He sat proudly for the moment, reminiscing on a time when he could infiltrate the nightlife, and not only fit in, but actually stand out amongst the crowd. Although those days were gone, he could still pretend for this single night. He, Gray Taylor, was going out on the town.

"So he asked if I'd go with him to the Village Tavern. He really is a great guy, Mom. I wish you could meet him." He sat explaining his plans to Sylvia.

"I really don't want you to think I'm selling you out, Mom. I'm going to be back in just a few hours."

He kept staring at her. He had a strong feeling of guilt. Though he knew she wasn't even hearing a word he said, he still felt overcome by betrayal. She wouldn't leave him alone.

'So, I'll see you around 10:00? Does that work for you, Mom?" He continued staring at her. "Great. I'll see you then."

He leaned over to give her a good-bye kiss. Right before planting a kiss on her forehead, he said, "Wish me luck, Ma. I haven't been out in public in half a decade."

He gave her a kiss and touched her hand.

'See you soon, Mom. I love you."

He turned and walked out the door.

Words of Wisdom

The Yellow Bird cab came to a slow halt outside the Village Tavern, and Gray reached into his pocket to pay his fare.

"That'll be $11.40," the cabby said.

"Man, you boys sure do know how to jack up the prices these days, don't you," Gray uttered sarcastically as he started counting the bills.

"Hey, buddy, I don't make the rules; I just follow them."

"I know. I'm just messing with you. Here, here's seventeen. Keep the change." Gray handed the cash the cabby's way, and the cabby in turn accepted it with a perplexed look on his face.

"Uh, okay, buddy. You have a good meal now, ya here?" he said, shifting to a more grateful tone.

"Yeah, man. Take care."

With that, Gray shut the door, and the driver pulled out and headed down East Centennial St.

As Gray walked to the entrance of the restaurant, he debated whether giving the guy nearly a six dollar tip was worth it. The guy had, after all, gotten a quick attitude with him. He just figured, *"What the hell. How often do I get out."* He let the thought go and continued to the door.

As he walked past him, he nodded at the doorman, whose nametag read "Julio." The first thing he saw as he got inside, waiting for him by the bar, was none other than the Colonel, dressed up in a sporty pair of Irish Linen pants, complemented by an off-white shirt of the same material. The old man looked great.

"You clean up well for an old guy, Rose," he said, as he patted the old man on the back.

"Well, from time to time we old guys need to show these pretty ladies just how they came into this world."

Gray laughed at the comment. "I suppose you do."

The Colonel took one last sip of his drink and stood. "What ya say we get a table?"

Gray glanced around the room. Back when he had been a regular at the restaurant, you had to put your name on a waiting list at least forty-five-minutes long to be seated. Now, there were empty tables all around the room.

As they followed a hostess to their table, the Colonel said to Gray, "Sure is nice to see you wearing something besides that same pair of jeans and that old jacket."

Gray laughed at the Colonel's cut. "Yeah, I wear that same outfit everyday. I don't really get home too much."

"Hardly even noticed that," the Colonel said mockingly.

"Yeah, well the only person I have to impress can't even open her eyes, so I'm not too worried about it."

The Colonel ignored the comment. "So what's your favorite dish here?" He picked up his menu, freshly handed to him by the hostess.

"It's been so long I don't know if they even still have it," Gray said as he grabbed his own menu out of the hostess' hand. "Let me see really quickly."

"What is it you are looking for, sir," the hostess asked, overhearing the conversation.

Gray looked up at her, noticing for the first time that she was, in fact, a very attractive girl. She had dark brown hair, green eyes, a tan complexion, and though not gentlemanly to notice, a great set of breasts.

"Well, Jennifer," he replied, as he read her nametag. He spoke in a flirting tone that hadn't been exercised in years but still somehow came forth naturally. "I used to really like this chicken marsala plate you used to have." He continued staring at her.

"Don't worry, sir. We still have it." She smiled. Her interest in Gray was evident. "That's my favorite too." She smiled again and then walked back to the front of the restaurant.

"And you said you've been out of the game for ten years."

Gray shrugged sheepishly. He too realized this attractive female was interested in him.

"Oh come on, kid. You can't just shrug that one off. No one who's been out of the game for ten years can snap back into form like that."

"Well, I just did. So let's forget about it and order."

"Well, whatever. That was impressive."

Gray snickered. "So what are you going to get?" he asked.

"Not sure yet. Probably ribs. They have great ribs here."

"Yeah, so I hear," Gray started. "I never really did ever acquire a taste for ribs. But I know my dad used to love them. He used to go to Earl's every Saturday and watch college football, eat wings, and then order ribs for dinner." He paused. "And of course, drink his fair share of draught beers too."

The Colonel laughed. "Sounds like my kind of man."

Gray nodded. "Yeah, I believe you guys would have gotten along really well."

"So are you a beer man, Taylor," the Colonel inquired.

"No, I gave up drinking right after the accident."

The Colonel nodded.

"Besides, even if I was still drinking, there's no way Ravel would let me bring a six pack up to Mom's room."

The Colonel laughed. "You mean, Dr. Ravel?"

"The one and only."

He laughed again. "Yeah, he is pretty serious all the time, huh?"

"Yeah, only thing he has ever talked to me about is taking Mom off life support."

Gray looked up to see what the old man's reaction would be.

The Colonel sat back in his seat. He was calm and collected. "Yeah, I've been having to speak with him about the same thing."

Gray was shocked. "You never mentioned that your wife was in a coma too."

The Colonel smiled. "That's because you never asked. I was letting you do the talking. You looked like you needed to talk about it way more than I did. I'm comfortable with it, myself."

Gray was speechless.

"How can you be comfortable with it, Colonel? This is your wife we're talking about here. Your soul mate. You can't just let her die."

The Colonel chuckled.

"Death is just a part of nature, Gray. Even though I wish there were something I could do about it, I can't. God has a plan for everyone. Now, it seems as if it's His plan for my wife to go be with Him very soon. I can't help that."

Gray couldn't believe what had just been said. He knew the Colonel claimed to be a Christian, but he didn't figure him to be one to put everything off on God's plan and timing.

He hated people who put things off on "God's plan."

"Yes the hell you can help it, Colonel." Gray was offended.

"Oh really, and how's that?" The Colonel asked, almost laughing at Gray's immortal stand.

"You don't let people like Dr. Ravel talk you into cutting her lifeline- that's how. You sit by her bed all day, every day. You sleep with her at night. And you sit there until she fights through it like the strong woman you know she is. Then, when she finally does, you walk out of the hospital with her that day."

The Colonel laughed. "Gray, Gray, Gray." He chuckled again. "So strong but yet so naïve."

Gray slouched back in his seat.

"I can tell you're not a religious man," the Colonel said.

Gray shook his head. "Not one bit. And I don't see how you can be either."

The Colonel smiled, not phased by Gray's comment. "Well, all the same, there are certain truths you have to accept."

"Such as?" Gray snapped quickly.

"Such as that whether there is an omnipotent God overseeing this world or not, death is inevitable. It isn't like your mother is the first person to ever have cancer. You told me yourself that the diagnosis was that her cancer was malignant, right?"

Gray slowly nodded his head.

"Cancer claims millions of people's wives and mothers every year, Gray. We aren't the only two people in the world going through this. Heaven help you if you are that self-centered to believe so."

Gray tilted his eyebrows just enough to indicate he indeed wasn't that self- centered, even though at heart he knew he was.

"Your mother and my wife are lying in a hospital room, completely lifeless. A recovery would be the worst thing in the world, Gray. Don't you realize that? The cancer would still be there. It's not going to magically, 'disappear.'" The Colonel mockingly shook his hands in the air like he was a magician.

"You see, Gray, whether you know it or not, God is calling your mother home to be with him. She has performed her duties here on earth." He sighed.

"It is your job now to relieve her of her misery and let her run free."

Gray had heard enough. He was so sick and tired of hearing about God and his natural plan and how all things work together for good. It was all religious propaganda that some liar named Paul had convinced everyone to believe thousands of years ago. Screw Paul, and screw anyone else who was apt to follow his ludicrous teachings.

The thing that scared Gray, was that for the first time, someone had made sense in a moral stand. The old man had made some quality points that Gray couldn't deny. Even though Gray didn't believe what the Colonel had to say pertaining spirituality, the part about Gray being self-centered and the idea that even if Sylvia was to be revived, she would be miserable- now that, unfortunately, made a lot of sense. He had to change the subject. He was not allowing someone to attack some sudden vulnerability.

"So, let me tell you what happened to me today." Gray decided to quickly change the subject.

The Colonel sat quietly for a second as he decided whether or not he was done lecturing the boy. He decided to concede. "I'm all ears."

"Well, right after you and I had lunch, I went back to the hospital to sit with Mom for awhile."

The Colonel nodded.

"Suddenly, I heard a knock at the door. I was alarmed because no one really ever knocks." He paused. "We don't exactly have a tremendous number of visitors."

The Colonel took note of the fact that Gray looked a bit sorry for himself. "Go on."

"Well, I opened the door, and guess who was standing right in front of me?"

"I don't know- Mary?"

"No, Renee!"

"You mean the ex-fiancée you told me about?"

"Yep. The one and only. How ironic is that?"

"Wow, very. Didn't you say you hadn't seen or heard from the girl in nearly ten years?"

"Not so much as a word."

The Colonel looked astounded. "So, what'd she say?" He seemed eager to hear the details.

"At first she tried to say a casual 'Hello,'- like we were still friends or something."

"And then?"

"And then I told her she couldn't just waltz into my mom's room like that. I told her she had no right."

The Colonel looked perplexed. "You didn't even allow her to explain why she was there?"

Gray was surprised by the Colonel's reaction. He assumed the Colonel would back his behavior. He stuttered a bit.

"Well, no. I mean, I told her she had to leave. But she did interject by saying she still loved me." He stopped in order to see what the Colonel's reaction would be.

"And you said?"

"Well, I scoffed at her and asked her again to leave."

The Colonel shook his head in disagreement. "Why on earth would you do that, boy?"

Gray didn't know what to say. He couldn't believe the Colonel didn't agree with him.

"Because she left me, that's why. Why does she have the right to come back now and say she loves me?"

The Colonel smiled at Gray.

"All this built up rage," he said, laughing at Gray.

"I'm glad you find this so humorous," Gray said. The old man was starting to offend him.

"I'm sorry, kid. I tell ya what- let me ask you one question." He paused to give weight to the question.

Gray raised his brow, signaling he was ready.

"Do you still love her?"

"What do you mean? That was ten years ago."

"I mean, do you still love her?"

"She left me, Colonel. She left me all by myself."

"But do you still love her?" He spoke slowly, sounding out each word in the sentence.

Gray attempted to defend himself again, but stopped.

"I don't know," he finally said with a sigh.

"Okay, now we're getting somewhere. So you don't know."

Gray shook his head.

"Well, then tell me this. What was your initial reaction when you saw her at your door?"

Gray thought for a moment. "I guess I was excited," he said quietly.

"So there you have it, son. You still care for the girl, whether you want to admit it or not."

Gray said nothing. He just stared at the wall for a moment. Finally he spoke up. "So what are you suggesting then?"

"I'm suggesting you hear the girl out on what brought her to see you today. And I suggest you take heart to what she has to say."

"You really think?"

"Yeah, I really think. All things happen for a reason, Gray. You need to open up your eyes and realize that doors are opening in your life, not closing. You are purposefully seeing things backwards, and if you don't act quickly, you may forever regret that."

"But, Colonel, she *left* me."

The Colonel paused as he stared Gray in the eyes. Finally he spoke up. "That may be, son. But blessings don't come through pride; they come through forgiveness."

Gray thought about that for a few seconds.

"So what should I do."

"You should eat dinner and then go over to her house. That's what you should do."

"Well what about you? What are you going to do?"

The Colonel smiled. "Don't you worry about me, Taylor. I have to meet my partner anyway. We have some business to take care of."

Gray was shocked at the sudden twist in his evening plans. In his heart he felt a strange, old feeling. It was the feeling of excitement. "Well, okay. I guess, if you think that's best."

The Colonel smiled again. "You think it's best too; you just aren't quite ready to admit it yet."

More Sweet Whisperings

Mary walked into Sylvia's room. As she flicked on the light, she was shocked that she didn't find Gray sitting at her bedside. This was the first time since Sylvia had been in the hospital that Gray hadn't been by her bed when Mary walked in for final check up. She smiled at the thought that maybe Gray had found someone to spend time with. She felt so sorry for the man, having no one to turn to but his mother.

She checked Sylvia's heart rate and frowned, knowing that it was only the man-made machine keeping her heart pumping. She put the liquid food in the proper place so that the tube would feed it to Sylvia. Finally, she knelt down beside her bed, held her hand, and offered her voice up in prayer.

"Lord Jesus, I bring this special woman before you. I pray your will be done in her life. May your angels be stationed around her and peace be with her internal thoughts. I also lift up her son, Gray, to you, Father. May he be willing to let this woman who is so special to him, go on to be with you. And most importantly, Lord, may he come to rest peacefully in the knowledge of salvation through your son. I pray these things in Jesus' Precious Name. Amen."

As she concluded her prayer, she remained on her knees for a long while, just holding Sylvia's hand. Meanwhile, she continued whispering for God's help and guidance.

A Forgotten Teaching

Gray rode the entire way to Renee's house in complete silence. He was extremely thankful that the cab driver was not interested in creating conversation. He had way too much on his mind.

What would he say when he got to her door? What did the Colonel mean by blessings come not through pride but through forgiveness? Gray had no idea what was to come of his meeting with Renee. All he knew was that the meeting was only moments away. He stared out the window as the cab inched closer to Renee's house.

Finally they pulled up outside 16 Andrews Lane, and Gray reluctantly climbed from the vehicle and paid his fare. As the taxi pulled away from the curb and drove off into the night, Gray stood motionless, staring at the house that was once his home away from home. His entire body was tense. He fought the urge to turn and walk away. He had to see what would come of this situation. Slowly, he made his way to the front door.

He finally gathered the courage to push the doorbell, and as soon as he did, it began offering a chime of "Jingle Bells." He was reminded of the time when he made fun of Helen Starnes for her insistence upon using "Jingle Bells" as her chime during the holiday seasons.

He stood in the cold for nearly thirty seconds, staring at his breath, but not at all noticing the cold weather that was causing this to be possible. Finally, he heard footsteps.

As the door was pulled back, the wreath he had been staring at was replaced by Renee's face. She looked shocked, yet thankful. She smiled at him. "Come in," she said softly.

Gray slowly walked through the doorway and stood uneasily in the foyer. He didn't know what to say.

"Come on. Let's go i nto the living room," she said.

Gray nodded. "Is your mother home?"

"No. She's at Marilyn's for Bridge tonight."

"Oh."

Gray continued studying the house as he followed Renee to the living room. It had hardly changed a bit.

"So, how are you?" Renee asked as she sat down on the couch.

Gray didn't respond. He rubbed the couch and then sat down himself.

"The old familiar couch," he said, trying to break the ice with a joke.

"Oh, shut up," Renee said as she laughed. "It was a good spot for a first kiss."

Gray nodded. "I suppose so."

Renee attempted to create some idle conversation, but Gray all of a sudden decided to cut through the formalities.

"So why'd you come to the hospital today, Renee?"

She stopped what she was saying and suddenly got very quiet.

"Well, to see you, of course."

"No, Renee. I mean why now? Why are you here? You haven't called me or written me in ten years. What are you doing in High Point?"

Renee sat still. She didn't know if she should tell the truth or not, for fear that she may be rejected and hurt. Finally she determined the risk was worth it.

"Because I want to come home, Gray."

"What do you mean? You are home."

She touched his hand. "No, Gray. Don't you see? This isn't home. Home is what we dreamed it would be ten years ago. Home is you and I- together." She paused. "I want to come home."

Gray didn't know how to respond.

"Renee, why now? Why after all of these years? I mean, you had a choice. You're the one who chose to leave, not me."

Renee started bawling. "I know," she said as she sniffled. "But it's not because I didn't love you, it's because I was scared."

Gray was offended. "You were scared? For God's sakes, Renee! We were engaged to be married! When were you planning on telling me you were scared?"

"No, Gray. I was never scared of marrying you."

"Then what are you talking about?"

"I'm talking about that night, when you called me. The night you're dad and Claire died. You sounded awful. The things you said about doing to that man were horrible- and the way you spoke of how your mother was the only person who meant anything to you... Whether you knew it or not Gray, you made me feel meaningless that night. So I got scared. Scared of the man you might become and scared that I would never be able to live up to your mother. I felt like you had her on a pedestal and that I'd always be second best to you."

Gray listened quietly.

"But that's no excuse for my leaving you, Gray. That was terrible. It was the worst decision I've ever made, and its affected my whole life. I should have just told you how I felt, but you were demanding a decision that night. You sounded possessed, Gray. I was mortified. But I know now that I had nothing to be scared about." She paused. "And I'm sorry, and I want you to forgive me."

Gray's conscience nagged him. As he looked at her, she seemed so apologetic. He couldn't help but feel she had, indeed, made the right decision in leaving. Had she stayed with him, her life these last ten years would have been miserable. She was right. She never could have lived up to Sylvia after that night because he wasn't prepared to let her. And she had every reason to be scared of the violent threats he had made that night. A year later, those threats had become reality. As he sit watching her cry, he decided that he must tell her the truth.

"I have to be honest, Renee. You were right to feel that way. And the pathetic thing is I never understood that until just now. I *was* possessed that night, Renee. Those things I said that night, about Tanner Buckman, and how I was going to kill him..."

He paused.

Renee wiped the tears from her eyes and waited for him to continue.

"I did. I killed him, Renee." He stopped and waited for a reply, expecting the worst. Renee continued dabbing at her eyes.

"I know you did, Gray. Of course I know. As soon as I heard he was dead, I knew it was you."

Gray was shocked. As soon as Sylvia had testified to being Gray's alibi at the time of the murder, everyone had been convinced that he hadn't done it. Everyone knew Sylvia Taylor wouldn't lie- everyone except Renee. She knew Sylvia would have done anything in the world for Gray.

"I hated you for that, Gray. For years I held a grudge against the man you had become. But every time I tried to date someone or move on with my life, something in my heart wouldn't let me."

Gray felt convicted. He didn't know what to say. Finally, he broke the silence.

"So what made you come back, Renee? What made you change your mind?"

Renee smiled. "This is the most amazing story, Gray."

Gray was baffled. "What happened?"

"Well, two weeks ago I was hired to defend a man on a charge of murder in the first degree."

"Okay."

"Well, he was accused of killing the man that had killed his wife and daughter in a drunk driving accident."

Gray perked up as he began to piece together the similarity.

"The first thing I always ask my clients before I agree to represent them is whether or not they are indeed guilty. I promise them that by law I am not permitted to disclose the information, but I must know the truth so that I can have a clean heart about representing them. Most guilty people lie, but I can read in their eyes that they are guilty. Those are the ones I thank for considering me as their legal counsel but refer to someone else. This man,

Lattimer Perry, was different. He looked me straight in the eyes and said, "Yes, I killed that man."

Gray sat quietly, intrigued by the story.

"So I asked him why. I asked him why on earth he felt that he was permitted to kill a human being." She paused.

"I'll never forget his answer as long as I live. He said, 'Young lady, when someone takes away the most important thing in your life, there is nothing you won't do if you think it might take away a fraction of the pain. But in the end you'll find out you're only making yourself more miserable.'" She paused.

"And suddenly, it seemed to almost make sense. All this time I thought your killing that man was something you were proud of, like it was an accomplishment, but then when I saw the pain that was still in Mr. Perry's eye's, it dawned on me that you too probably felt that same pain. All you wanted was revenge."

Gray nodded his head slowly. That was exactly how he felt. He wasn't happy or remorseful for killing Buckman. He was simply miserable.

"So, when did you decide to come back down?" he asked quietly.

"Well, even though I sympathized with Mr. Perry, I explained to him that I couldn't defend him. But for the next week and a half, I couldn't stop replaying those words he said through my head. I continually tried to decide whether I should just press on with life or come down here and tell you how much I still cared for you."

"So what made you finally make your decision?"

"Well this is the amazing part, Gray. Bare with me here."

Gray nodded.

"After a week or so of debating it in my head, I had this sudden feeling as if I should read the Bible."

Gray grimaced.

"I know. I have always hated when people say to seek God for the answers to your problems. But you know what I found? There may actually be some truth to that."

"What makes you say that?"

"Last Wednesday night, at a colleague's recommendation, I decided to open my Bible. It took me a while to find, but I finally found it. It's the one your dad gave me the day I graduated high school."

Gray nodded, remembering the gift.

"Well I took it off the shelf, and dusted it off. Then I held it in my lap for a few minutes, debating whether I was ready to open it. Finally, I decided I was. Suddenly, I remembered your mother telling me that if I was ever seeking counsel from God, to pray over my Bible and ask Him to let me open the book to the passage he would have me read."

Gray chuckled, remembering the old teaching.

"And I remembered how she said that the key to making it work was believing God was powerful enough to do it. She said you had to have faith. So I made a pact with God. I closed my eyes and prayed. I said that I would open my heart and have faith in Him. I told Him I would believe in Him if the page I opened to really did give me the advice I was looking for. I remembered to close the prayer the way your mother always did, with "in Jesus' precious name I pray, Amen." Finally, I opened the Bible."

Gray saw tears slowly forming in Renee's eyes.

"You know what I saw on the page I opened to, Gray?"

Gray sat very still, anxious to hear what she was about to say.

"There, in the book of Psalms, was a picture of you hugging me that graduation night. And the very first passage I looked at was Psalm 17: 22. Do you have any idea what those verses say?"

Gray shook his head.

"They say :

The troubles of my heart are enlarged. Oh Lord, bring me out of my distresses. Look upon my affliction and my pain; and forgive my sins. Consider mine enemies; for they are many, and they hate me with cruel hatred. Keep my soul and deliver me: let me not be ashamed, for I put my trust in thee. Redeem me, Oh God, out of all my troubles.

As soon as I saw those words, I started bawling, Gray. There's no way of explaining that. That's not coincidental. That can't happen by pure luck. Don't you see, Gray? The passage is saying for God to take us both out of our distresses and our troubles but that the only way that can be possible is through forgiveness. So I felt like God was telling me to forgive you and that if I were to come home and confront you, then you too could forgive me- and then we would finally be redeemed from all our troubles."

Renee looked to Gray with hopeful eyes.

Gray sat quietly, not knowing what to say. He wasn't ready to believe that God had shown Renee the verse. He did, however, realize that it was quite ironic that she turned right to such a fitting verse and that it was doubly ironic because the Colonel had just finished lecturing him on forgiveness. He decided he didn't want to dwell on the thought but instead relish in the fact that the love of his life had come back for him.

"So what do you think, Gray?"

Gray still sat quietly.

"Gray?"

"I don't know what I think, Renee, but I do know one thing." He paused.

"From September 24, 1995, through "Til death do us part'- I will always love you."

A tear streamed down Renee's cheek.

Gray opened his arms, and Renee fell into him. Softly he whispered, "Welcome home, Renee."

Familiar Arms

Renee clicked the lock button on the key chain to her mother's Lexus. As it beeped she said, "Thank God Mom rode with Marilyn tonight or else we'd be at the mercy of the High Point Yellow Cab service all night."

Gray laughed. He picked up on the fact that the comment meant she was planning on spending more time with him that night. All of a sudden, he felt a familiar feeling of happiness as he realized he might just be getting lucky later on.

After Gray and Renee had spent thirty minutes embracing on the couch, Renee had decided that they go see Sylvia. Gray was extremely moved by the gesture. Renee's accompanying him to the hospital would allow him for the first to time feel as if he was not alone in dealing with Sylvia's demise.

The cold January evening stung their bodies as they walked from the parking deck to the entrance of the hospital. The distance was at least one hundred and fifty yards, so as they finally got to the front of the building, their ears and fingers were completely numb. As they walked through the sliding doors, Gray yelled a hello across the room to Merle and gave her a wink as Renee led the way to the elevator.

Merle smiled, "You go ahead with your bad self, Mr. Taylor!"

Gray laughed. "What's up, Merle?"

She winked at him. "That's my boy. You got you a good man right there, young lady."

Renee felt awkward and forced a smile. "Thanks," she uttered softly.

"You kids have a good one now, you hear?" The grin had yet to leave her face.

Gray laughed. "Night, Merle."

"Night baby."

They kept walking. "What was that all about, Gray?" Renee asked.

"Just a sweet woman with a sweet heart. That's all."

They headed down the hallway, onto the elevator, and climbed to the 6th floor. The doors opened, and Gray led Renee to room 613.

When they got to the door, Gray knocked, pretending he wasn't interrupting. He peeked his head into her room.

"Mama, guess who's come to see you?"

"Here she is," he said as he opened the door wider.

"It's Renee, Mom. She wanted to come visit you."

Renee stood uneasily as she stared at Sylvia's motionless body. She couldn't stop looking at all of the IV's and machines she was linked to. Earlier when she had come to talk with Gray, their fight had somehow blinded her to the terrible state Slyvia was in.

"It's okay. Go over to her," Gray said.

Renee slowly moved toward the bed. Gray followed behind her.

"It's okay. Say hi to her, Renee."

Renee felt very uncomfortable.

"Gray, I don't mean this offensively, but she can't hear me."

Gray patted his mother's arm. "Sure she can. Can't ya, old girl?" He smiled and winked at Renee.

"Uh, hey, Mrs. Taylor." She didn't know what else to say.

"Yeah Mom, I went over to her house tonight. Remember how I told you I was going to meet that nice old man? Well, I told him about how Renee showed up today while you and I were talking, and he basically told me I was an idiot for telling her to leave. And you know what? He was right. We had a great talk just now."

He looked up at Renee and smiled.

"And so I decided to go over to her house. When I got there, she told me how much she loved me and couldn't live without me. And she told me how I was the greatest person on earth, and how much of an idiot she was, and..." Renee cut him off.

Laughing she said, "That'll do, babe."

Gray smiled back at her. He continued to stroke Sylvia's arm.

"I missed you, though, Mom. Did you miss me? That's the first time we've been apart for more than an hour and a half in over five months."

Renee watched with pity as Gray spoke to her.

"But don't worry, Mom. Renee was taking good care of me. You'd be proud."

He paused.

"Except she did kiss me when we were at a stop light. I told her you were my best girl, but she just kept right on kissing. She wouldn't take her hands and lips off me, Mama!"

Renee smacked him with her purse.

"That's not true, Mrs. Taylor. Your son kissed me!" She laughed.

Gray smiled up at her, thanking her for amusing him and pretending like Sylvia was actually taking part in the conversation.

"You should have seen her, Mom. She was cramming her tongue down my throat. I could hardly breathe."

"No way, Mrs. Taylor. He was begging to kiss me. He wouldn't let go of the gearshift to let me put it into drive until I gave him a little peck."

The two kept laughing as they flirted back and forth like third graders. Finally, Renee looked at Gray with a mischievous twinkle in her eye.

"Do you mind if I take your little baby home with me tonight, Mrs. Taylor?" she looked at Gray the whole time she spoke. His eyes were locked with hers.

"Yeah, would you mind, Mom?" He turned to look at Sylvia. He smiled as he rubbed her hand.

"I think you'll be all right here for one night by yourself."

He started getting quieter, realizing he was leaving her by herself overnight for the first time since she had fallen into her coma. He glanced back up at Renee. God, she was beautiful.

"I'll be back to see you first thing in the morning, Mom. I promise." He smiled and rubbed Sylvia's arm for a few more seconds, and then he stood up and put his arm around Renee.

"Come on. Let's go," he said as he motioned her to the door. She followed his lead.

Just before reaching the door, Renee turned back and said, "Before we leave, I just want to thank you for teaching me long ago the importance of faith. We wouldn't be here together if you hadn't insisted upon preaching that to me."

Gray didn't know what to say, so he just opened the door. They walked out into the hall and started down the hallway. Suddenly, he stopped, realizing he had forgotten something very important.

"Wait here, babe, I'll just be a minute."

He slowly walked back over and knelt at Sylvia's bedside. Softly he whispered in her ear, "Don't worry; you'll always be my best girl." He kissed her forehead, and turned and walked back out the door. As he shut it, he placed his arm back around Renee's waist.

"Okay, now I'm ready. What ya say we go make up for some lost time?"

Renee smiled. "Best idea I've heard in years."

As Gray pushed the lobby button on the elevator, he winked at her, "A decade to be precise."

Something to Believe In

The bright rays of the freshly risen sun danced across Renee's windowsill, and two young bodies lay intertwined beneath the covers. Two half-empty wineglasses sat on the nightstand beside them.

The bright light awoke Renee first, and she opened her eyes to face Gray in this way for the first time in years. She stared at his face. Her mind flashed back to when this was a normal wake up sight. She lay there for nearly five full minutes, just basking in the old familiar feeling of contentment. Finally, she whispered to awake him.

"Gra y. Gray." She ran her fingers through his hair. "Gray, baby, it's time to wake up."

Gray opened his eyes and then shut and reopened them again, as he tried to adjust to the light. Realizing that all of last night's occurrences hadn't just been some sort of amazing dream, he smiled and began rubbing her outer thigh over the sheets.

"Good morning," he said.

"Morning," she whispered back.

"Man, I've missed this," he said.

"Yeah. I was just thinking the same thing."

"You were just thinking of how much you've missed sleeping in a bed too?"

"Oh, shut up! You know what I mean." She leaned over and gave him a peck. "Punk."

He laughed. Then he rolled over the direction opposite Renee and reached his arms to the sky, yawning while he stretched. Then he sat up on the edge of the bed. He grabbed more blanket to cover himself.

"I need to get back to the hospital to see Mom," he said.

"Yeah. I need to run some errands with my mom, too. That is, if she's back yet."

She jumped from the bed and covered herself in her down comforter. She walked over to the window to see if the car of one of the bridge club ladies was in the driveway.

As she stood pulling back her curtains, Gray stared at her. The light coming through the window illuminated the down comforter, making her appear to be a porcelain goddess. God she was beautiful!

He continued to stare at her, until she finally turned around and said, "Yep, Marilyn brought her home. You can tell by the Porsche out there. That comes compliments of Dr. Stansbury."

They both laughed.

Marilyn Reynolds had been married three times, all unsuccessfully. The only benefit from her romantic misfortunes was the divorce settlement she received from her three-year fiasco with Dr. Martin Stansbury.

"Poor old bastard is funding half the High Point female population," Gray said.

"Wait. Don't forget Greensboro too!"

They both laughed.

Dr. Stansbury had been married over six times now, each divorcee taking every ounce of money she possibly could once she had caught him cheating.

"Well, here are your pants," she said, as she threw Gray's chinos to him.

"Thanks," he said, as he caught them in midair.

"So are you just going to hang out at the hospital for the rest of the day?" Renee asked.

"Well, that's what my everyday routine has been for the past month," he said, as he finished buttoning the last two buttons of his pants. He buttoned the top button then stopped and looked at her.

"Renee, can I ask you a question?"

"Of course you can, silly. What's up?"

"No, I'm being serious. This is a very serious question"

She wiped the smile off her face and sat straight. "Yes, of course, Gray. Anything."

"Are you going to be here for me?" He searched her eyes for truth.

"Yes, Gray. I'm here with you now, aren't I?"

"That's not what I me an, Renee."

He paused.

"I know last night things seemed to jump right back into place for us, but there's a lot we don't know about what has been going on in one another's lives these past ten years. I'm not the same man I once was. I used to be secure. I thought I was independent."

She sat quietly, nodding her head, implying that she was trying her best to follow.

"When Dad and Claire died and you left, I transformed into a whole new person, Renee. I bottled myself up completely. I shunned the rest of the world. The only person I clung to was Mom- because I truly believed she was the only person left in my life I knew I could count on."

Renee attempted to interrupt, but Gray talked over her.

"She was all I could depend on, Renee."

Finally he paused.

"I am facing a very tough decision, Renee- a very, very tough decision. And I just need to hear you promise me that you'll be there for me if I, indeed, opt to do something drastic."

Renee was confused. "Gray, I don't understand. What decision?"

Gray looked at her with the most stern, serious look she had seen on his face in the twenty-four years she'd known him.

"Just answer the question, Renee. Are you in this? Are you beside me? For better or worse…can I count on you?"

She looked him directly in the eyes. "Yes, Gray. You can count on me."

"Then that's all I need to know," he said, as he began walking to the door.

"You didn't drive over here, sweetheart," she said softly.

"Oh, yeah," he said, a bit embarrassed.

Renee giggled, not wanting to fully laugh at him. She could tell he was in a serious mood.

"Hang on just two seconds, sweetie; I'll get dressed and take you back to the hospital."

"Thanks," he replied sheepishly.

Hearing the Music

Mary sat by herself in the hospital cafeteria, drinking her morning coffee. She offered half-smiles to the two men who were seated at the table catty-corner her, as she realized they were watching her every move. She had grown quite used to being admired by all of the men since having worked in the hospital. In an effort to avoid any more unnecessary eye contact, she grabbed a newspaper and pretended to start reading.

The double doors to the lobby split open, and Gray walked back into his familiar surroundings. He smiled at Merle and made his way to the cafeteria where he was going to get his coffee to go. When he saw Mary sitting there, he decided he'd have his cup there instead.

"Hey, Mary," he said as he walked over to her table.

"Hey, Gray. I missed seeing you last night." She smiled up at him.

He smiled back. "Yeah, I ran into my ex-fiancée."

"Oh, do tell!" Mary said, putting her paper aside and sitting up in her chair. She looked at Gray with big eyes.

"Okay. Let me grab my coffee really quickly, and I'll fill ya in."

He headed over to the coffeepot, and realized, much to his chagrin, that today, unlike yesterday, the coffee was not fresh. He poured his coffee, added his cream and sugar, and headed back to Mary.

"So I went to meet the Colonel last night for dinner," he began as he sat down.

"The Colonel?" Mary asked, trying to follow.

"Yeah, that old guy I told you about my running into the other night."

"Oh yeah, yeah. The Rose guy."

"The one and only." Gray laughed and took a sip.

"So me and 'the Rose guy,' wer e sitting down talking, about to order, when I told him that my ex-fiancée had come by Mom's room yesterday."

"She had?" Mary was confused.

"Yeah, but that's a whole different story."

"Umm, okay," Mary said. Gray could tell she wanted details.

"Well, I told her to leave. I didn't even hear her out on why she had come to see me."

"Why would you do that, Gray?"

Gray shrugged. "I don't know. It made sense at the time. But what ended up happening was that the Colonel talked me into going to her house and sitting down and hearing what she had to say."

"And?" Mary was eager for details.

"And we got back together, Mary."

Mary's eyes lit up. "Gray, I'm so happy for you."

Gray grinned. "Yeah. I'm pretty excited myself."

Mary laughed, "I'll say. You're grinning from ear to ear."

Gray just smiled again. He took a sip of his coffee.

"Well then, I guess you guys were just 'meant to be.'"

"Well, normally I'd laugh at you for that comment, Mary, but maybe that is the case. I mean, you know I don't believe in fate or destiny or any of that stuff, but maybe there are certain things in this world that are, in fact, meant to be." He took another sip of coffee and sat back.

Mary recognized vulnerability in Gray for the first time ever. She sat forward, and uneasily said, "Gray, there's something I've been meaning to talk to you about."

The look in Mary's eyes indicated that she was about to speak of something serious. Gray became alarmed.

"Is something the matter, Mary? Is it Mom?"

"No. Well yes- I mean, your mother is fine." She paused. "I mean for the time being that is."

Gray got defensive. "What are you trying to say, Mary?"

She sat still for a moment.

"Gray, I've been wanting to talk to you about this for weeks now. And I know this is a topic you are very cold toward, and I pray you will not hate me because I'm bringing it up."

Gray just sat listening quietly. He didn't know quite where she was going.

"Gray, I've been looking in on your mother for over a month now. I also have had seven cancer patients in that time period." She paused, knowing what she was about to say was going to be very hurtful.

"Two of them were recovering from surgery. Four of them passed on." She paused again.

"Your mother is the only one left, Gray. And I don't really know how to say this tactfully, so I'll just put it bluntly."

Gray just sat stunned, listening. His heart thumped rapidly in his chest.

"Gray, she's not really here anymore either. She is essentially gone already, and she will stay that way for as long as you keep her on Life Support."

She paused. She knew how much this must hurt to hear.

"She's never going to recover, Gray. Even if she miraculously did, she wouldn't ever be happy. She has cancer, Gray. Cancer. She's ready to go now." She stopped and let a few moments pass by. "And now it's up to you to just let her."

Gray sat quietly as he stared at the table. He knew it was true. He had, in fact, been pondering it all morning. He didn't realize just how serious it was, though, until hearing it come from Mary. Hearing Mary say this was much different than hearing it from Dr. Ravel. Mary had been there for Sylvia everyday since she fell into her coma. She wouldn't just allow

Sylvia to pass on unless she truly didn't stand a chance.

Mary had finished her thought and was eager to see whether Gray would either lash out or start crying. When he did neither, she was shocked. Instead, he just sat there, quietly, as if he was thinking things over. Finally he spoke up.

"You know, Mary, I have realized that to be a fact. I know I have to let her go, but it's not as easy as it seems to everyone else. You see, I always have felt that if I were to let my mom go, I'd have no one. Not a single person to cling to." He paused.

Mary didn't know what to say, but luckily Gray continued talking.

"But last night, after spending time with Renee," he stopped as he tried to gather his thoughts. "I think we are getting back together, Mary."

Mary sat up in her seat as she realized what Gray was implying.

"I really think she's going to b e here for good this time, Mary. I really do."

Mary broke in. "That's great, Gray. I'm so happy for you."

Gray nodded. "Thanks."

He kept talking.

"But still, letting Mom go is the toughest decision I'll ever have to face. I don't even know if I will be capable of loving anyone once she is gone. She's all the love I've ever known." He stopped and looked at Mary. "So you'll have to give me some time to think things through."

"Of course, Gray. I wasn't trying to imply that it needed to be done right now. I just wanted you to know how much it has troubled me lately. Plus, I wanted you to know all of the facts."

"Well, I appreciate it, Mary. I appreciate what you've done for both my mother and me throughout the course of this past month."

He paused.

"You have been like an angel, Mary. I mean that. I'm not a religious person, but that's all I can fashion you to. You've been amazing."

She smiled at the compliment. "It's certainly been my pleasure, Gray."

Gray smiled and then downed the remainder of his coffee. "Well, I need to get up there to see her."

Mary nodded. "I'm coming up that way in a few myself."

Gray stood to leave. As he walked to the trash can to drop off his coffee cup, he continued to replay Mary's words through his head.

Another Simple Song

The elevator doors opened, and Gray walked down the sixth floor hallway en route to Sylvia's room. He had mixed feelings of guilt and fear as he neared the door. He felt as if leaving his mother alone last night was some form of betrayal, and he was overcome with fear as he pondered the idea of letting her go. Slowly, he opened the door and walked in.

"Hey, good looking," he said softly, not in the boisterous manner he had always greeted her with before. "How's my girl?" He sat down in the chair beside her and began stroking her arm.

"How did things go without me last night, Mom? Were you okay?" He continued looking at her. Now as he looked at her, he didn't see the strength he had convinced himself he saw this past month. Now he saw a feeble, dying woman who was ready for her time to come. He had never felt so empty in his life.

"Renee and I had a good time last night, Mom. Wasn't it great to see her again?" He kept rubbing her arm.

"Yep, she sure is something. I didn't realize how much I'd missed her until she walked into the room yesterday afternoon." He attempted a laugh. "I tell ya what, Mom, I've never been more shocked to see someone in my life." He laughed again. "I can't believe how rude I was to her." He stroked a few of the strands of her gray hair and then tucked them back behind her ear.

"I'll tell you another thing- she sure couldn't have come at a better time."

He paused.

"I'm not doing so good, Mom. I'm confused. I'm lonely. I don't know what I feel about anything anymore. My mind's going in a thousand different directions, and I feel like I'm losing it. I honestly think I'm losing my mind. I mean, I'm surrounding myself with absolute strangers and actually taking their advice on the most serious decisions of my life. Suddenly, I'm talking to strangers about things I wouldn't even talk to you about, and I don't even understand why. God, I just don't know what's going on in my life anymore."

He paused.

"I just wish you could wrap me up in your arms like you used to do and tell me that everything is going to be alright- I wish you were here, Mom."

He smiled at her.

"You know, I sometimes wonder, Mom. I mean, I used to believe in God- but now I don't. But you never did give up. Dad and Claire never gave up either. So if there is a heaven somewhere beyond here..."

He paused, trying to collect his thoughts.

"I wonder if that means you'll be able to see them once you're gone. You know? Like the people who all believe in the same God go to the same heaven or something. That's what I try to tell myself. I try to believe you will be happy with Dad and Claire again, if I let you go. That you won't have any pain, the way you used to tell me that Dad and Claire didn't have any pain anymore when they died. God, I hope you're right."

He paused, just sitting- thinking.

"I know they would sure love to see you."

He continued to stroke her arm.

"I think Renee and I will get married, Mom. I think I may have a family of my own sometime soon. I sure wish you could see them."

He chuckled softly. "There would never be a case of more spoiled grandchildren on the planet."

He sighed, knowing her fantasy of playing with her grandchildren would never come to fruition.

"Well listen, Mom, I'm going to go grab a quick smoke and then call Renee. I'll be back up to see you in a little while." He patted her arm and then stood to head to the door. He blew her a kiss as he walked out. He headed down the hallway and onto the elevator.

As the elevator finally dropped him off on the lobby floor, he made his way out to the front, ducking Merle and Jamie who were in mid-conversation. He didn't feel like conversing at the moment. He had bigger things on his mind.

He zipped up his jacket as the cold outside air hit his body. He reached into his back pocket, finding that he only had two cigarettes left in his pack. Soon, he'd be back to smoking a real cigarette again.

Just as he put the second to last stick to his lips, he heard an old familiar voice say, "I know you're not going to be stingy with that last fag, boy."

He wheeled around to see the Colonel, grinning at him from ear to ear.

"Hey, Colonel," he said quietly, as he extended the final cigarette to him. "Did you get things squared away with work last night?"

The Colonel nodded his head. "Yeah, I think we're finally starting to make some progress."

Gray exhaled. "I don't think you ever told me what it is you do."

"Human Relations. My partner and I have been working with a specific kid for awhile now, and it looks like things are finally taking shape for him."

Gray flicked at his cigarette so the superfluous ashes would fall from the stick. "I wish I could say the same for my life."

The Colonel looked at him questioningly. "Well, did you go see the girl last night?"

Gray nodded.

"And?"

"And things went really well; I ended up staying at her place last night."

The Colonel smiled. "Okay, so then why the long face, kid?"

"Because my Mom's dying, Colonel; that's why!"

The Colonel took a step back as Gray lashed out at him.

"Whoa! Easy there, Taylor. Why do you say that like it's a surprise?"

Gray didn't answer. He dropped the cigarette on the ground and crumpled it with his boot. He stared up at the sky.

"Taylor, I'm talking to you, son. What is the problem?"

"I'll te ll you the problem, old man. The world is the problem. She's dying. She's dying, and I can't stop it. And I don't know if I'm ready. Okay? I don't know if I'm ready to let go."

Gray's voice was strong, and the Colonel didn't want to interrupt just yet.

"And God is my problem, Colonel. God drops these blessings on certain people, and then he does nothing but take from me. I mean, what the Hell? And now, suddenly, Renee wants to talk about faith? I don't know if I can deal with that, Colonel. I mean, until I am given some type of blessing, I'm not going to ever acknowledge any God."

The Colonel finally jumped in.

"You know, for someone who claims to not believe in God, you sure do cast a whole lot of blame on Him."

Gray was offended. "What do you know, old man? You're just a simple old guy who's never had to worry about anything until now. You got to live your whole life with your wife. Your kids never had to experience losing their loved ones. It's easy for you to preach on the goodness of God. He's never messed with your perfect little world."

The Colonel had heard enough.

"You want to know what I know, you ignorant, naïve little punk? I know that standing before me I see a great kid, a great kid with a loving heart. But you're so damn busy concentrating on casting all your life's troubles on God that you don't ever take a look around you. You speak of blessings. You say you haven't had any blessings in your life. So then what do you call that woman lying up on her deathbed? Huh? What do you call that? Do you know how many kids go through life never even having a mom? Or worse, one that doesn't even love them? You spent nearly thirty-five years having a concrete, loving relationship with your mother. And if that wasn't enough, you have a beautiful young lady who loves you and wants to spend the rest of her life with you. So don't you tell me I don't know anything. And don't you ever tell me that God doesn't bless us because you have been abundantly blessed, and it's high time you grew up and realized that. No one said this life was easy, Gray. But it's the way that you face adversity that causes you to grow and get through it."

Gray was taken aback. He started to cry.

"But Colonel, I don't know whether I am even capable of loving once my mom is gone. If she dies, I don't know if I'll be strong enough to ever love again."

The Colonel stood quietly and watched as Gray stood weeping. Finally, he spoke up.

'Son, I know you're hurting. And I know you don't want to acknowledge God's existence. But if you're crying because you're scared your ability to love will die when your mother dies, the Bible is where you need to be looking."

Gray looked at the Colonel through tears. "What are you talking about?"

'I'm talking about songs, Gray. I'm talking of a sweet, sweet melody. In the Bible there is a simple song that will guide you through your mother's death."

"What song?"

"The Song of Solomon, Gray. Read it. Chapter eight, verse six. You'll see what I mean. Just trust in God for once, Gray; He will see you through this."

With that, the Colonel dropped his cigarette on the ground and started walking away.

"Where you going?" Gray asked quickly.

He didn't even turn around. He just answered back over his shoulder, "I have to go prepare things for my wife. Tonight's the night."

Gray couldn't believe he hadn't even mentioned that he was letting his wife go in a few hours. "What do you mean tonight's the night?"

The Colonel nodded as he kept walking. "Yep, tonight's the night."

"But wait, how can you just…"

"Song of Solomon 8:6," he said over Gray's attempted question.

"But you're not even going to…"

"Song of Solomon 8:6," he repeated once more.

Gray gave up and just watched him walk back into the building. For the first time, he realized why he was so drawn to the Colonel. Just like with his father, he knew he had seen something in the Colonel that inspired him, something he wanted to have in his life. Finally, he knew what it was: he wanted his faith.

Quickly, Gray ran into the hospital. He was on a mission- a mission for something he never would have thought he'd need. He was on a mission to find a Bible.

A Quest for Wisdom

Merle was reading the day's <u>High Point Enterprise</u> as Gray walked up to her desk.

"Didn't you used to write for this paper, Gray?" she asked as she saw him approaching her desk.

"Yeah, many moons ago," he answered quickly.

"I sure do love this paper," she said. "I wouldn't know what was going on in the world if it wasn't for this."

"Yeah it's a good publication."

Merle could tell Gray was fidgety. "What can I do for you, baby?"

"Merle, you go to church, right?"

"You better believe it. He's Risen Family Church. I'm a Deaconess."

Gray smiled. "That's nice. Do you by chance have a Bible back there?"

Merle smiled. "Well, yes I do. It's not my personal Bible, but they require us to keep one back here in case someone like yourself needs it."

It was an awkward moment, and Gray felt embarrassed. He quickly grabbed the Bible from her.

"Thanks, Merle," he said as he walked quickly toward the elevator.

As the elevator climbed to the sixth floor, Gray started flipping through the pages, trying to figure out where Song of Solomon was located. He didn't have a clue whether it was even in the Old Testament or the New. Finding it could take hours.

The doors opened, and Gray walked quickly to Sylvia's room. He let himself in and then shut the door behind him.

"You'll never believe what I'm doing, Mom. I'm actually reading the Bible."

He looked back down at the book. "Now, if I can only find what I'm looking for."

He continued to flip the pages of the book for a full ten minutes, all to no avail. He had seen the book of John at least seven times, and Genesis and Exodus at least twelve times respectively. Why couldn't the verse be in one of those books? Why did it have to be Song of Solomon? He was becoming frustrated. He looked to his mom.

"How am I supposed to find this stupid book, Mom? I mean, there's like two thousand pages in here, and I don't even know where to start looking." He stared at her as if she could answer him.

Finally, he flipped to a page that read "Song of Solomon" in the top right corner. Quickly he flipped to the next page, which is where chapter 8 started. He found verse six and started reading to himself. What he read shocked him. The words simply read:

"Set me as a seal upon thine heart: for love is as strong as death."

His body trembled. He stared at the words, and marveled at the power they possessed. The Colonel was right. This simple song truly did hold the answer he needed.

He would forever be able to love. To Gray, Sylvia was love. Thanks to the Colonel, he now realized that love was as strong as death. He wept. He sat weeping for nearly a full minute. As he wept, he remembered the revelation God had made to Renee. God had told her that forgiveness was the key to having all of your sins redeemed. He now knew the final act he must perform before letting Sylvia go: he must forgive.

Forgiveness

He stared at the letter in his hand for a minute before deciding to indeed send it. Finally, he licked the envelope, sealing its contents inside.

Gray had just written a letter of apology to Lincoln Buckman, confessing his guilt for killing his father. In the letter, he tried to provide the advice that Lincoln's bitterness about his father's death would bring him nothing but heartache. Though he was scared to go through with mailing the letter, he knew in his heart that it was the right thing to do. He knew that because of double jeopardy laws he couldn't ever be tried for Tanner's murder again. He licked the envelope one more time and then handed it to Merle to mail out that afternoon.

"Thanks, Merle," he replied, as he handed her both the letter and the Bible.

"You're welcome, baby. You find what you were looking for?"

"And a whole lot more," he said with a smile on his face.

"Good. Is there anything else I can do for you?"

"Actually, yes. Can you page Dr. Ravel?"

"Of course. What do you want me to tell him?"

"Just ask him to meet me in my mother's room, would you?"

"Sure thing."

"Thanks."

Gray smiled and walked back to the elevator.

Once he was back in the room, Gray sat in his seat by Sylvia's bed but didn't even offer a word. He just watched her.

Much to his surprise, it didn't take Dr. Ravel long at all to get to the room. He knocked softly and then turned the knob and entered.

"You needed to see me, Mr. Taylor?" Gray could sense that he seemed a bit perplexed.

"Please, call me Gray. And yes, I did."

"Well is there something I can do for you, Gray?"

"Well actually, I asked you to come up here so I could apologize."

Dr. Ravel couldn't believe his ears. "To apologize?"

Gray nodded. "I have treated you so disrespectfully this past month, Doc, and I am truly sorry. I know there is no excuse for my behavior, but please let me try to explain. It's just that I am very close to my mother, and I have had a really hard time dealing with the fact that she is dying."

"I know. I have always understood that, Gray."

"But that's still no excuse for my behaving the way I have toward you. You were only trying to help, and I was taking all of my frustrations out on you. And I wanted to say that I am sorry."

Dr. Ravel stood quietly. Finally, he smiled. "Well, apology accepted, Gray. No harm, no foul."

Gray paused for a few seconds. Dr. Ravel could tell that Gray had something else on his mind.

"Also," Gray started and then paused.

"Yes?"

Gray stood quietly. Finally he whispered, "I'm ready."

Dr. Ravel was shocked. He thought he would never hear those words come out of Gray's mouth.

"Are you sure, Gray?"

Gray looked at his mother. He stared at the tubes that were connected to her body. She looked so pale. He nodded his head. "I'm sure."

Dr. Ravel nodded. "Well then, I'll make the arrangements for tonight. Mary and I will come up at 7:30."

Gray nodded.

"If I were you, I'd spend these last few hours right in this room, Gray. But then again, I already know that's exactly what you'll do."

Gray forced a smile and nodded.

Dr. Ravel shook his hand and then walked back out of the room.

Gray turned and faced his mother. As he walked back over to his chair, his heart was tied in knots. How was he ever going to be able to say good-bye?

A Difficult Good-bye

The time was going on half- past seven, and the sun had set nearly an hour earlier in the world outside the hospital window. Gray had spent the entire day in the old, familiar chair by Sylvia's bed. He had spent every minute of that time staring at his mother, attempting to capture her beauty one final time. As he looked to the alarm clock on the counter, the red numbers indicated the time had come. Dr. Ravel and Mary would be coming any moment.

Finally, a soft knock came at the door and was followed by Dr. Ravel and Mary walking slowly into the room. They both offered smiles of consolation, and Gray in return tried to offer a smile of his own.

Dr. Ravel put his hand on Gray's shoulder. "You ready, Gray?" he asked softly.

Gray looked to him and studied his face for a second. He then looked to Mary. He closed his eyes and flooded his mind with a picture of Renee. Softly, he nodded his head. "Ready."

Dr. Ravel nodded at Mary and started walking toward one of the machines Sylvia was hooked to. Until this very second, Gray hadn't even known which one of these machines was the one keeping his mother alive.

"Just take your time, Gray," he said quietly. "Tell me when you're ready."

Gray looked at him and nodded. He looked over at Mary. Tears ran down her cheeks. She tried to force a smile, but it was too late. Tears fell from Gray's eyes. He looked at Sylvia.

He paused for nearly twenty seconds, twenty seconds that felt like twenty hours. He searched his mind for the proper words to say. Nothing was coming to mind. What could he possibly say at a moment like this? He looked up to Dr. Ravel. Through stifled tears he asked, "Doc, with all due respect, is it possible for me to be alone to do this?"

Dr. Ravel looked at him uneasily. He then looked at Mary, as if she could give him the proper advice. Mary nodded her head, signaling she thought he should, indeed, let him.

Dr. Ravel pondered it for a moment and finally spoke up. "Gray, you know I'm not supposed to do this."

"Please, Doc. I will never tell a soul. I just don't feel right with anyone else being here when I say good-bye to her. It was always just us against the world, and it needs to end that way."

Dr. Ravel clasped his hands and put them to his lips as he stood thinking. Finally he said, "All right, Gray. But you can never say a word about this to anyone, you hear?"

Gray nodded at him. "Thank you, Dr. Ravel. This means the world to me." Mary stood smiling. Tears streamed from her eyes.

"Okay, come here, and pay attention as I show you what you have to do."

Gray stood up and walked over to Dr. Ravel.

"It's very simple," Dr. Ravel started. "You just flip this switch right here, and that's it." He looked up to see if Gray had followed.

"That's it?"

"Yep, that's all there is to it, Gray."

Gray nodded and then stuck out his hand. As Dr. Ravel shook it he said, "It's been a pleasure, Gray."

Gray peered into his eyes. He couldn't escape the conviction for how awfully he had treated him. He pulled Dr. Ravel into him and held him for a few seconds. Through tears he said, "I'm sorry, Doc. A million times, I'm sorry."

Dr. Ravel patted Gray's back. "Don't even mention it."

The doctor then pulled away and walked over to Sylvia's bed. He softly whispered, "May God bless you and keep you, Sylvia Taylor."

Mary looked at Gray, her eyes indicated she wanted to say a few quick words herself. Gray motioned her toward the bed.

Mary walked slowly, and what she did as she got to the bed shocked Gray. The moment she got within a foot of the bed, she got down on her knees and softly lifted her voice in prayer. Gray would never forget the words she uttered:

"Lord Jesus, I bring this special woman before you one final time. I pray her soul would be prepared for the celebration you have in store for her, the celebration that will take place in just a few moments. Thank you for her loving son. Thank you for opening his heart to being willing to let his mother go on to be with you. May you bless her and keep her, as she is reunited with the ones she loves. In your name I pray, Lord. Amen."

She stood and touched Sylvia's hand a final time. She then looked to Gray. He stood stunned, speechless. Mary walked over to him and gave him a hug. She then leaned back and kissed him on his cheek.
"She is going to be just fine, Gray. I promise. She'll be in good hands."
"Thanks, Mary," he whispered softly.
Dr. Ravel and Mary headed out the door. As the door closed, Gray walked back over to his seat by Sylvia's bed.

He sat quietly for nearly a minute as he held her hand in his. Tears were rolling down his cheeks, but he was determined to fight them back long enough to say his good-bye. With as much strength as he could muster, he wiped the tears away from his face.
"Well, here we are, Mom. You and me, just like it always was." He gripped her hand a bit more tightly.

"You know, life's funny, Mom. As a kid you think things will be the same forever, that growing old is so far away. I..."

He tried to keep speaking, but tears again started trickling down his face.

"I never thought this moment would come, Mom. I never thought I'd have the strength to allow it." He paused.

"You are the only thing that has ever kept me going. You don't know how many times I have thought back and reflected on the times we have shared, on the things you have done for me. I can honestly say that there is no other mother I know that has loved her son the way you have loved me. I am the luckiest kid in the world."

He smiled at her.

"You remember that time Mrs. Sheffield accused me of lying about being sick so I could miss her test?" He laughed at the thought. "No other mother in the world would have stood up to her the way you did, Mom." He paused again.

"Yeah, life sure is funny. It was only two days ago that I wouldn't even listen to a single word about letting you go." He paused. "I was so hardheaded, Mom. I wouldn't listen to anyone. I treated people so badly. You would have been ashamed. But I did it all because I felt like you were the only thing I had left in my life." He wiped more tears from his face.

"But suddenly, it's as if my heart was magically opened. You should see the way Colonel Rose deals with the fact that he's about to lose his wife. Its amazing, Mom. It's truly amazing. The faith the guy has is unbelievable. He told me something today that I will never forget as long as I live. He told me that I have been so busy trying to blame my bitterness on God, that I haven't even acknowledged the blessings in my life. I have thought about that long and hard, Mom, and I realized what my blessing is. It's you.
I have been so blessed to have someone love me as much as you have. There are so many people in this world who have had to go through a whole lifetime never receiving love from anyone. And then there's me: a kid who has been showered with the deepest love possible. And all the while, I have been too self-centered to even be thankful for it. And I'm sorry, Mom. I'm so sorry."

He paused.

"But I finally see how I am supposed to reward you. My gift to you is to go on to be with the God you love so much, the God you speak so highly of.

Last night I said a prayer for the first time in ten years, Mom. I didn't address it to any God in particular, I just prayed. You know what I prayed? I prayed that you would be with Dad and Claire again, that you could hug your Mommy and Daddy. I prayed that there truly would be no more pain in the heaven you've always spoken of.

I just want to say I'm sorry, Mom. I'm so sorry I kept you here longer than you wanted to stay. You're my reason for being, and you're my reason for living. I am everything I am because of you. You're my hero."

He continued gripping her hand. Tears were pouring faster now, as he knew the final moment was about to come.

"You remember when Claire was a baby, Mom? When you took me to the movies? Do you remember the promise I made you? When I promised that I'd never let you die?" Tears now soaked his face.

"Well, you were right, Mommy. Death is just a natural part of life. It can't be avoided. I tried. Oh, God, I tried so hard. But now it's time; it's that time you promised me had to come. It's finally here, and we are living it right now.

I don't want you to worry about me, Mom. I'm going to be just fine. Renee and I are going to have a family of our own. I'm so sorry you never got to see your grandchildren. I promise they will know how special a woman their grandmother was. I promise."

He paused.

"She's going to take good care of me, Mom; don't worry. Renee will take good care of me." He continued crying.

"But there's one thing I told her last night that I want you to know. I told her that you are and always will be my best girl. Forever, Mom. Forever and ever you will always be my best girl."

He stood to his feet. Tears covered his face. He leaned over Sylvia's bed and planted a kiss on her forehead.

"I love you so much, Mom. I love you so much and I will miss you."

He continued to whisper how much he'd miss her. Finally he pried himself away. He held her hand for a final time and simply said, "Thank you for everything, Mom."

He took one last glance at her and then headed toward the machine. As he got behind it, he whispered softly to himself, "I love you, Mom," and then he lifted his voice in song.

Though the words were soft and simple, their message said it all:

'Somewhere beyond here, amidst the shining stars, someone's watching over me- caring from afar. Somewhere beyond here, someone's resting in God's arms, asking Him to bless me and keep me safe from harm. Somewhere beyond here, where angels dry your tears, someone's waiting for me- somewhere beyond here."

He sang the song the entire way through, and as he sang the final words, with tears flooding his eyes, he flicked the switch.

Familiar Faces

"And I will dwell in the house of the Lord, forever," finished the pastor of Hopper Ave. Baptist Church, as he concluded with the funeral reading of Psalm 23.

"And now, Sylvia's son, Gray, has a few words he would like to say."

Gray made his way to the pulpit and spread a few notes out before him. He looked up and scanned the crowd. What he saw nearly brought him to tears. He saw the faces of all of his high school friends. He saw the faces of all of his college friends. He saw all of the friends he had made from his various athletic days, all sitting in the pews. He saw co-workers from the <u>High Point Enterprise</u>. He saw old teachers and coaches. He saw Renee. He saw Colonel Rose. He saw Mary. Nearly every person Gray had ever been close to was sitting in the crowd. He looked back down at his notes and began to speak.

"You know…"

This was all he got out. He looked at his notes again and then folded them up and put them back in his pocket. After a brief silence, he spoke back up.

"I spent nearly five hours last night writing down what I wanted to say this afternoon." He paused. "But I'd rather just say the first thing that comes to mind."

He looked into the audience and fixed his eyes on Felix Hay, his college roommate who had come all the way from Oklahoma. He looked next to him at their friend Thomas Heery, who had apparently made the trip from Pennsylvania. Tears began flooding his eyes. His entire group of college friends was seated beside one another, all intently waiting to hear what he had to say. He nodded thankfully their way.

"You know, I don't need notes to talk about what my mother meant to me. I don't need a rehearsed speech on why she was an amazing woman because, as she used to say, the 'proof is in the pudding.'"

"I look out around this crowd of people, and I see friends I thought I had cut ties with nearly a decade ago. People I have been so cruel to that have apparently loved my mother and me regardless. And I thank all of you."

He chuckled.

"That's right, the proof is in the pudding."

He continued nodding his head in positive reinforcement.

'She always told me that the company one keeps is indicative of the person they truly are. As I look out at this crowd, I see what must be the most loyal, loving friends a person could ever have."

He stood quietly for a second and then softly uttered, 'So I guess that means at one time I was a loyal and loving person."

'So what is love? You can't see it. You can't hear it. Oh, but you can feel it.

But what is it?

Now let's see. It's a four-letter word. That's right, it's just four simple letters. It's short. It's not hard to say. Yet the whole world revolves around it.

Yes, this simple word is the most important word in the English language, and the critical act of expressing it was taught to me by one special person. It is she who we come here today to honor."

"You see, there was a difference in the way Sylvia Taylor loved people. Sylvia Taylor loved people unconditionally. She didn't care whether you were white or black, whether you were poor or rich. It didn't matter who you were or where you came from. She would love you regardless."

He paused and then laughed. "But, boy, did she love me."

The crowd all chuckled, as they all were witnesses to the fact that Sylvia Taylor prided herself especially in Gray.

"She was the kind of mother who always showed her children how much she cared for them. The kind of mother who stood behind her child when he had made a mistake, rather than being ashamed that he had been a bad reflection on her." He paused. "Those are the good mothers."

"I want to say an apology to all of you who I didn't even bother calling to let know she was ill. And for those of you who banned together to get the word out about today's funeral, I am forever grateful. But I have a confession to make."

"For the past ten years I have been a cynical man. For whatever reasons, I believed that my mother was the only pure thing I could count on in this world, and as I look at all of your faces, I know I was wrong. But please, let me explain."

"Ever since I was a child, my mother and I have shared a special bond. We always got along better than a normal mother and child. She was my inspiration. She was the bar by which I measured who I wanted to become. When my father and sister passed away, I saw just how fragile life was. I then decided that I needed to spend all the remaining moments we had with one another."

"Which was all fine and dandy. But the mistake I made was in feeling that I needed to share that time with only her. I realize now that I am responsible for creating all the demons that have held me down for so long."

He paused and chuckled.

"But the whole point of this long-winded story is to say that in the end, the solution to all of my problems was simple. I realized that I needed to appreciate the type of love my mother had for this world and then put that kind of love to practice in my own life. And I have a very special man to thank for teaching me this lesson."

He winked at Col. Rose. "Colonel, I will never take her love for granted again."

The Colonel nodded at him.

"Life is short, people. It truly is short. Let's not let a lifetime pass us by, living it without love."

"Please, don't cry for my mother. I believe she is in a better place now. I'd like to believe she is with Claire and Dad, looking down on me as I speak right now. And because I have accepted by faith that they are watching me right now, I know my mom is singing a special song to me.

Because it is known to all that I can't carry a tune, I will just say the words back to her, but I must conclude with a promise I made to her when I was six."

With that he looked up to the sky. "I'm thinking of you right now, Mom, missing you." He smiled as he pictured Sylvia smiling back down on him and then began, once again, reciting those special words.

As he finished and had uttered the last word- though known not to be customary for a funeral- the entire crowd stood to their feet. They stood clapping for nearly a whole minute. Tears welled in Gray's eyes.

"Thank you; thank all of you."

As the clapping ceased, he saw Felix Hay stand from where he was sitting.

"Gray, would you mind if I said a few quick words about your mother?" he asked.

"Of course not, Felix," Gray replied.

Felix began addressing the entire congregation.

"Sylvia Taylor was like a second mom to me. It wasn't easy going to school all the way across the country, leaving all of my loved ones behind. She always made me feel like I was a part of the Taylor family. The day I met her I realized how special she truly was. I witnessed that special love Gray just spoke of, and from that moment on, I was hooked. She was a special lady to all of us, Gray."

He paused.

"And I just want you to know that she instilled that same love you speak of inside of you. Every person in this room surrounded themselves with you because you loved people in that same way. I'm very sorry about your loss. You are right, though; she truly is in a better place."

As Felix concluded, he nodded at Gray, reemphasizing his point.

"Thank you, Felix; thank you so much."

As soon as Felix had sat back down, Kenneth Hall stood to his feet. "Yeah Gray, I'd like to say something about your mom too."

After Kenneth finished, another stood to his feet, then another, and more following that.

A full hour had passed before the final person had stood to praise Sylvia Taylor. Gray had sat down long ago, and tears of appreciation had streamed from his eyes the entire while.

Finally he stood up and walked back to the pulpit. He whispered into the microphone, "Thank you all. I could never ask for more than this."

He stopped for a moment and then concluded with an even lighter whisper:

"I love you, Mom."

Reunion

Gray smiled as he parked Sylvia's old BMW in her space in the driveway. Sylvia had always loved her BMW. She refused to let him sell it, even after she could no longer drive it.

The car had hardly been utilized since she had been forced into her wheelchair. However, every once in awhile, when the mood was just right, Gray would take it for a spin. As he'd drive, he smile as he'd reminisced about the old days when she'd come zipping into the driveway and park in her favorite spot under the big oak tree. It was this same reminiscence that was causing him to smile now. He put the car in park and opened his door.

"This is the old house, Mary," Gray said as he opened the rear door for the nurse. He was delighted that she had asked to have dinner with him and Renee.

"It's beautiful," Mary replied. "Whose rope swing is that?"

Gray looked over to the oak tree, and stared at the faded yellow rope that hung from one of its branches. He smiled again.

"That was Claire's. Dad rigged that swing for her when she was five."

Mary flashed a big smile. "I'm sure she must have loved it." She stared at it a bit longer. "Can I have a quick swing?"

Gray shrugged. "Uh, I guess. Just be careful."

At that time, Renee had finally finished putting on her lipstick in the front seat and exited the car to join the conversation.

"You should have seen how often Claire would swing on that thing when she was young," Renee said. "Every time I'd come over here she'd be out there with Jack, swinging until Sylvia called them in for dinner."

Gray laughed as he remembered the days as well. He put his arm around Renee and gently rubbed her shoulder. They both watched as Mary placed her foot in the foot hole and carefully swung from the branch. She screamed in delight as she flew through the air. Finally, she removed her foot from the rope and joined the other two.

"What ya say we all go in and have a bite to eat?" Gray said.

Both women nodded their heads in agreement.

Gray led the party into the house and flicked on the lights. As the lights came on, Renee led Mary into the kitchen, while Gray stood in the hallway staring at the old photographs on the wall.

As he continued looking at all of the old pictures, he felt a feeling of contentment. He smiled as he looked at the pictures of Jack holding Claire the day she was born. He nearly broke into laughter as he looked at the picture of Claire dressed up like a fitness instructor at the age of three. Finally, he sighed as he looked at the picture of Jack, Claire, and Sylvia, all hugging at Claire's eighth grade graduation. Inside, he prayed that they were all together, just like the picture, at this very moment.

"What are you looking at, sweetie?" Renee walked up behind Gray and put her arms around his waist.

"Oh, just pictures. Just remembering things, that's all."

"Are you okay?"

Gray thought about it for a second and then smiled. He nodded his head. "Yes, I do believe I am." He turned around to hug her.

"Wasn't that exciting how everyone was at the funeral today?" Renee asked.

Gray nodded his head. "It was overwhelming."

"It was so great to see some of those people," Renee started. "I haven't seen Felix in twelve years. He hasn't changed a bit."

Gray chuckled. "No, he sure hasn't." He thought to himself for a moment and then sighed. "You know, I have some amazing friends, Renee."

Renee nodded. "The best."

Gray smiled. "I sure wish you could have met the Colonel, though. He has been so important in my life these past few days. Honestly, if it weren't for the Colonel, you and I would not be standing here right now. You'd probably be back in Boston, and I'd still be at the hospital." Gray sighed. "He's an amazing guy, Renee."

"I wish I could have met him."

Gray sighed. "Well, at least you have gotten to spend a little time with Mary."

Renee nodded. "She's as great as you said she was. I can see why you felt so comfortable with her."

"Yeah, she's an awesome lad y. I really don't know what would be going on in my life had she not been Mom's nurse."

Gray was interrupted by a knock at the door. Both Gray and Renee turned quickly toward the sound, and then looked to one another.

"Did you invite anyone over?" Gray asked Renee.

"No, are you not expecting anyone?"

Gray shook his head. He began walking to the door. "I have no idea who it might be."

He opened the door and was shocked as he saw the Colonel standing before him.

"Colonel? What are you doing here?"

Colonel Rose smiled. "You took off today before I got a chance to say good-bye."

Gray was confused. "Good-bye?"

The Colonel disregarded the question and let himself in. He walked past Gray, and suddenly Renee was able to get a look at the man.

"Douglas?!" Renee exclaimed, recognizing him.

"Hello, sweetheart," he said, as he walked over and gave her a hug.

Gray was completely confused. "You two know each other?"

Renee was equally confused. "This is the nice old man I told you about from the airplane."

Gray looked to the Colonel for him to provide some explanation. Instead, the Colonel just kept smiling.

"It sure is good to see you kids back together," he said. The smile had still yet to leave his face.

Gray was trying to formulate the proper question to get an explanation of what exactly was going on, but before he could come out with it, the Colonel kept speaking.

"You know, a miracle happened in my life last night, Gray."

Gray, still confused, responded with a half-hearted, "What?"

"I got my wife back."

Gray couldn't believe his ears. "You mean she pulled through?"

The Colonel nodded his head. "Yep, that's exactly what she did, son. She pulled through."

Gray smiled. "Well I'm glad to hear it."
He paused.

"But would you mind telling me how you were on a plane with Renee and you were with me at the hospital on the same night?"

Renee fixed her eyes on the man, also intently waiting the answer.

The Colonel just smiled. "Yep, she pulled through. And she's here, she wants to see you."

"She's here?" Gray was stunned.

"Yeah, she'll be right up. She was just looking at that BMW out in the driveway really quickly- she was really taken by it."

"Uh, okay," Gray uttered, not quite sure what to say.

Just then, Mary came walking back into the hall where they were all standing.

"Mary, this is the guy..." Gray began.

"Hey, Daddy," she said over Gray, very nonchalantly.

"Hey, sweetheart," the Colonel said, as he gave her a big hug.

"Whoa, wait a minute," Gray said, his confusion mounting.

"Daddy? You told me you didn't even know who he was."

Mary smiled. She too gave no reply. Renee and Gray stared at one another, completely at a loss for what was going on. Suddenly, a woman appeared in the doorway.

"Mommy!" Mary screamed as she saw the woman.

The woman just stood very still, smiling at Mary, as if she hadn't seen her in a very long time. "Hello, baby."

Mary ran over to her and gave her a huge hug.

"What is going on here?" Gray demanded.

As Gray spoke up, the woman relinquished her hold of Mary, and looked to Gray. She smiled. She stared at him for what seemed like an hour. Finally, she walked over to him.

"Hello, Gray."

Gray looked at the Colonel's wife. She was beautiful, remarkably beautiful actually. He continued staring at her. Moments went by, and still he was watching her. He was captivated by her. He couldn't remove his gaze from her eyes. They gave him the most eerie feeling. It was just like with those of the Colonel. He had the feeling as if he'd known her his whole life. Finally, he extended his hand and said, "Hi, I'm Gray."

She shook his hand and said, "Of course I know who you are, Gray."

"You do?" Gray asked quickly. He could feel that something almost surreal was going on, but he just couldn't quite put his finger on what it was.

"Of course. Thank you for everything." She leaned in and gave him a hug.

Gray hugged her back, all the while feeling extremely uncomfortable.

The Colonel spoke up. "Gray, I was telling my wife about that novel you told me you started so long ago."

Gray let go of the Colonel's wife and looked to him. "Yeah?"

The Colonel's wife broke in. "I think that's a marvelous story, Gray. You must finish it."

Gray was taken aback. "You think?"

"I know. Trust me. It will mean the world to me. You have to promise me you'll finish it."

Gray didn't know what to say. Why would it mean so much to her? Suddenly, Gray realized he had never mentioned the novel to the Colonel.

"But I never..."

"Do you promise, Gray?" the Colonel's wife spoke over him.

Gray looked her in the eyes. Though he didn't know why, he responded, "Yes, I promise."

She smiled. As she smiled, he began to feel more as if he knew her.

"Well, you three ready?" the Colonel asked.

Mary nodded. She walked over and kissed Gray on the cheek. "I'll see you soon, Bubby."

Gray jumped back. "What did you just call me?" Suddenly things were starting to click.

Mary smiled. She walked over again to hug her mother.

As the woman opened her arms, she said, "Yessy Mommy's little baby girl. Yes you are. Yes you are. Mommy's missed you."

Gray couldn't believe what he was hearing. Could this be? Could this really be happening?

"Well, son, you truly are a fine young man," the Colonel said. "I am indeed proud."

"But wait..." Gray had so much he wanted to ask, but the Colonel kept on talking.

"We will see you sometime soon, Gray. But until then, you have a life to live. And until then, just remember that simple song. Love truly is as strong as death, my son."

Tears started falling from Gray's eyes.

"And the same goes for me, Gray," his wife said. "Just remember one simple song. And I pray you will always hold on to that song."

Tears now poured from Gray's eyes. He nodded at her. Softly he said, "I love you, Mom."

She smiled. "We have to go now, Sweetie. But I will see you again, my little Queege. I will see you again sometime soon, in a world somewhere beyond here."

She winked at him. As he watched her he wondered how he hadn't pieced it all together the first moment he looked in her eyes, or in the Colonel or Mary's eyes for that matter.

"Come on, Sylvia, he'll be just fine," the Colonel said as he pulled her toward the door.

"We love you, Son," he said as they began to walk away. "And remember, love is as strong as death."

As these words were spoken, the three turned to walk out the door. Gray followed after them, trying to get in a final word, but as he followed them, they disappeared into the January afternoon.

Gray just stood weeping. Renee had walked over to Gray and had grabbed him in a tight embrace. Finally, Gray wiped his eyes and looked up to her. He smiled and grabbed her a little more tightly.

"I love you, Renee."

Epilogue: Completion
September 2066

Completion: It is completion I have always found myself striving for in this life. Finally, I feel as if my life indeed has reached that point. This causes me to sigh.

Faith led me to begin this story, and it is only through faith I was able to finish. The arthritis in my fingers stings badly, and my body does not enjoy sitting in this upright position for so long. But I knew God would help me through the pain. And He did.

So now my final promise has been fulfilled. And as I look back on eighty-four years of life, I realize promises are one of only two things that got me through it: promises, and songs.

The angel of my father once sang me a simple song.

His song taught me that love is as strong as death. And he was right. Nearly everyone who was ever close to me is now gone. Friends, family,... even Renee. But as I prepare myself for my final exit, I cling close to the remembrance of them all. As

I do, my heart beats a little faster as I am reminded of the love that I will always have for them. Yes, love truly is as strong as death.

And then there's one other song that has guided me through life. It's a song I wake up singing and then hum to myself as I fall asleep at night. That song, of course, is my mother's song.

So much has changed since the day she took me to the movies so many years ago, but one thing hasn't. When I look up at that big star-studded canopy in the sky, my heart still wonders if my mother and I truly are wishing upon the same bright star. This thought always forces me to smile, knowing she is looking down on me from wherever she may be, loving me and being proud of the man I have become.

That, friends, is the promise she made me.

My story is now complete, as nearly is my life. Through the years I have been attempting to write this story, I have debated what I might do with it upon its completion. I have prayed about it many times, and have come to the conclusion that this story is not for everyone to hear. Rather, it is meant to be shared with a very special few. So to whoever finds himself reading this, remember one thing: live, laugh, and love, and most important of these- love.

I stare at my keyboard one final time, as I know it will not be touched again after this last paragraph. Therefore, I know I must choose my words wisely.

I know that someday soon, the sun will set on my final day, and I will fall asleep for the final time. As I arise the next morning, I will open my eyes and realize I am in a whole new place. It will be a place where there is no pain, a place where there are no time constraints. And wherever this place might be, I know beyond a shadow of a doubt, I will see my family again--- in a world somewhere beyond here.

ISBN 141201223-6